A Twist of Faerie

K M Jackways

Published by Old Souls Press, 2024.

A catalogue record for this book is available from the National Library of New Zealand

ISBN

[978-1-0670250-3-8] (kindle)

[978-1-0670250-4-5] (paperback)

Sign up for the author's newsletter on the website to be the first to hear of new releases: www.kimjackways.com

Chapter 1

Cara

At Halloween, when the dead leaves are taken into the ground and the veil is thin, it is said that a whisper can echo through worlds.

"Trick or treat!" The kids' voices screeched.

"Here, have the rest of the bowl." Cara felt sorry for the children, who were just on the edge of growing up and looked a bit awkward. Some had made a half-hearted effort to dress up as pirates. She waited until they'd taken handfuls of wrapped lollies, then shut the door lightly.

"That's my good deed for the year," she said, catching her sister's eye. "And a blessed Samhain to them. Now we can ignore any more knocks. Unless it's that hot fireman I've been waiting for. I'd definitely get the door, then."

Serena smiled. "You're a witch," she said. "You should be able to make it happen."

Serena was four years younger than Cara, but looked nowhere near her 29 years, with her clear skin, large eyes above ruddy cheeks and long fingers resting lightly on the bench, as if she could float off the earth at any point. Serena's long, fine, blonde hair contrasted with Cara's own heavy brown bangs that never sat right. They couldn't look more different.

"It doesn't work like that," Cara reminded her. "Witchcraft is subtle and you have to tease it gently, not force it to your will. I'm not looking, anyway. No one will ever live up to the male characters in books."

But three wines later, she found herself mixing up a potion. She threw in sage, rosemary and, of course, mustard seed.

"It was once called eye of newt, you know," she said, over her shoulder.

"I do know. That smells good," her sister said, reaching her hand toward the cauldron.

"Careful." Cara said it automatically. Looking out for her sister was as much a habit as scratching her nose. 'Take your sister along,' her parents used to say. 'It will make her happy'. So she took Serena with her to her drama class, to her friends' houses after school, to her first job at the supermarket.

Serena was a crying, colicky baby. As soon as she touched the cot mattress, she cried. She wouldn't lie down. She couldn't sleep. She was too small, too pale. She wouldn't grow, wouldn't feed. She scratched at her head with tiny fingers and left red, raw lines. Cara saw her mum grow drawn and stressed, and her dad became snappy and gradually spent more hours at work.

Then when Cara came into her powers in her teens, she was able to see what was wrong with her sister. She learnt about potions, adding herbs to her sister's meals for fatigue and trouble sleeping, and ground up plant powders for concentration. She gave her potions for reflux. She experimented with salves and ointments to help her itchy skin. It helped a little, but there were new symptoms each week.

Serena had been to so many doctors and they always told her that she should get better in a few months. Her life had always been a delicate balance between being social and preserving her energy.

"Oh well, at least we lasted longer than last year's Halloween party," Serena said, pulling a blanket around her shoulders.

"Lottie understands. And witchcraft is the perfect end to the day. Come on then, write your wish on this piece of paper." She pushed the notepad page and pen towards her sister.

Serena raised her eyebrows at the engraved fountain pen. "Does it have to be a fancy pen?"

"No, witchcraft doesn't depend on that. But I have to use them some time. What should I save them up for? Letters from my death bed?"

Serena shrugged. They often used gallows humour to deal with the fact of Serena's illness and her sister was a master of the dry retort. "Might be nice."

"Alright. Quick bit of housework." Lifting her palms up and curling them slowly into fists, feeling the power build in her forearms and wrists, Cara sent it out towards the dirty dishes, which wiggled and jumped into the dish rack, perfectly clean.

Serena laughed. "Goddess, that one never gets old," she said with delight. "If only I could do that. It's so unfair that I get the chronic illness and you get the witchcraft!"

"Well, that's why I'm here for you." Cara said, lightly. "Now, let's get on with it."

"You are," Serena replied, tilting her head to one side. "What shall I ask for, then?" Her sister held up her wineglass and swished it around. The liquid caught the light, as if whole worlds were caught inside the glass. Ruby worlds with crimson trees.

Cara knew what her sister would write. For the last few years, Serena had been desperate for a family of her own. At one point, she had a partner. Matt. They had moved in together, and were happy for a while, but they eventually broke up. Serena arrived at Cara's tiny flat in Ledstow village, pale and drawn, and moved into the little room upstairs. Her sister would wish for a family.

"Perhaps someone will be listening one day," Cara mused, out loud.

What about her own wish? Cara visualised a strong, sexy fireman who treated her like a princess. One who stayed to share breakfast and understood the love language of funny memes. Wouldn't that be lovely?

She sighed one of those full-body sighs, put her own pen to the paper, and finally wrote the same wish as ever. It was what she had been whispering every first star of the evening and each time she blew out the candles on her birthday since she was young: 'I wish for my sister to live a long, healthy life.'

"What are you huffing about?"

"Oh, nothing. Tonight feels like a good time for a re-watch of Practical Magic."

Cara dropped the pieces of paper into the cauldron, where they disappeared with a flash of light and a sizzle, and reached for her glass of wine.

THE NEXT MORNING, CARA woke up late. She wrapped herself in her dressing gown and wandered out to the kitchen. Serena was nowhere to be seen, but there was a piece of note paper on the bench. 'Gone to get bread x' was written across the page in Serena's light, curved hand. The kitchen smelt of cleaning liquid and there was no trace of last night's drinking and witchcraft.

Her phone alarm buzzed at her and Cara looked down at the screen. The planting! Lottie had made her promise she would turn up to the tree re-planting as a representative of the coven. It started ten minutes ago.

After the quickest shower known to womankind, Cara threw her clothes on. Pulling her coat around her, she grabbed her phone, before stepping into her gumboots and sloshing across the wet leaves. The horse chestnut tree outside brought shades of gold and bronze to the grey, damp day.

She stopped at the corner supermarket before ascending the windy road. "Have you seen my skin and blister today?" she asked Nigel, the old man at the counter who knew everyone in town.

He reached under the counter for his 'Closed' sign and stretched to place it at the end of the conveyor belt.

"Ah, yeah, as a matter of fact," he said. "Serena was talking to that lad who just started here for work experience. Think he was stocking the shelves. Tall, skinny fellow who really thought the world of himself. Haven't seen him again this morning, either."

"Right," Cara had said, slowly. Her protective instincts were already stabbing at her spine, but she made herself relax. Serena was an adult. She'd lived by herself.

When she arrived at the planting, the others were about to drop their saplings into the holes dug for the trees. The local newspaper photographer was standing nearby, with his camera on a tripod.

The town lay below a clinging fog this morning; Ledstow, her first love, a town whose bricks were spread with the mortar of love and protection. She could see the church steeple and the top of the oak trees around the cemetery peeking from the cloud. Cara waited until the photo session was finished, drawing her coat in the autumn chill.

People came to Ledstow for a new life. Some of them passed through the library, and she helped them with whatever they needed. She didn't ask a lot of questions. They turned up in town because they needed a haven. They had nowhere else to go or nowhere else they wanted to be. But the cloak of protection only extended so far, and there were those who resented the magicals and non-magicals living in harmony. It was up to her and the other witches in the coven to protect the town's peaceful state. Mostly, that meant keeping up the protection charms and keeping tabs on any suspicious activity. But the coven worked together with other community groups as well.

Today, it was tree planting. Suspicious fires last season had left the hillsides burnt and bare, and the coven agreed that it was the right time for the new saplings to be planted.

"But why does it have to be me?" she grumbled, under her breath. "I've got books to shelve. Fingerprints to clean off windows."

"Where's your sister?" Dave McMillan, a school teacher and the head of the Ledstow Improvements Society, asked her. He leaned over to where a variety of digging implements were stuck into the soft grass.

Cara found a spade thrust into her grip. "I'm not sure. She said she was going to turn up."

"She went right past earlier. Well, it looked like her, at least."

Cara made a face. Up here? Serena would be safely down in town, somewhere, surely. But she had a twinge of uncertainty, not quite fear, at the top of her spine.

After working for about an hour, digging into the soft earth, gently wriggling the saplings out of their plastic bags and nestling them into their holes, Cara sat down for a rest at the edge of the plantation. A felled branch made a practicable seat and she lay her coat over it. Her stomach gnawed at her.

She pulled out her phone to ring her sister. Perhaps she could pick up some lunch for them on the way back.

The phone went straight to voicemail.

She stood up to try ringing again and noticed a flash of white. It appeared to be a snowdrop, fragile and elegant. Past that was a clump of daisies, then bluebells, and then an old-fashioned hellebore, or winter rose. She followed the curious trail of flowers, glancing behind again as the hush and fresh scent of the trees enveloped her. Had someone scattered a wildflower seed packet through here? She wasn't complaining. The flowers were a welcome distraction.

At the end of the trail were bright red Scarlet Elf Cup fungi, looking for all the world like they were holding their vessels up to be filled, and a line of toadstools beneath a tree covered in moss. She bent down to look, making sure not to get too close. Vague cautionary tales ran through her mind of fairy rings and kidnapping.

"I'm not that naive," Cara said, in a low voice, to no one in particular. "There's no way you'll catch me stepping into—"

The world fell away from beneath her feet in a sickening lurch.

Falling, dropping, lost.

She flailed for an instant, in the between, as something resisted. Then she came through and her hand went up to her face as she landed at the edge of a lake so shiny it hurt to look at.

"— a fairy ring." Her voice came out in a whisper. "Oh, goddess."

In the other direction, she squinted to see that the plantation was gone and the forest around her was old and overgrown with moss and lichens. Huge tree trunks stretched to the sky and vines swung between them. Wild flowers crept between the trees; bluebells, daisies, and some large blooms she couldn't name. She smelt a musty scent, like the pot pourri in her grandmother's dresser.

The light had a sort of purple quality as if she was looking through tinted sunglasses. A waterfall streamed into the lake opposite her. Where was she? If she knew one thing, it was that this was not Ledstow. Not even England. The autumn damp feeling in the air was gone. She jumped up and looked carefully around.

A faint silver shimmer, like very fine glitter, hung over the ground where she had landed. A fairy tale. She was in a cursed fairy tale.

She walked back and forth over the spot, looking for the portal that she'd come through, then leaned back against a wide trunk. Her phone was nowhere to be found. Alright, this was fine. Fine.

An unfamiliar bird called a three-note call. Shadows were starting to creep through the clearing, and she shivered. Sitting at the edge of what looked like a large, forbidding forest was a silly thing to do. How many times had she railed at the main character in fantasy books for making stupid choices? She just needed to make a plan.

Water. She headed back towards the lake, bent down and scooped some cold water into her hands. Was it her imagination or was that the best, freshest water she'd ever tried? Perhaps a hint of melon...

"What are you?" A woman called from behind her. "And what are you doing in the Auld Forest?" The voice was friendly enough.

Cara turned. The Auld Forest. That answered the question of where she was, although it didn't help her much. The dark hood of her coat covered half of the woman's face and she had two small children, who were huddled behind her, clutching at her skirts.

"I'm a librarian," she said, rubbing at the spot on her hip where she had landed. "I didn't mean to end up here."

"Folk often don't," the woman said, and turned away.

"Wait. Please. I don't know how to get back."

"You can't. That way was just closing when you fell through."

"Yeah," one of the kids said, obviously feeling a little braver, as she came out from behind her mother. Fair hair framed a round face with pointed ears and large, round eyes. "Everyone knows that."

Cara approached the family. "Thank you," she said, to the child, with a kind smile. "That's what I was worried about. Do you, perhaps, have a map?"

The child shook her head.

"No, we don't, but there are only two directions," the woman said, still speaking loudly as if Cara was hard of hearing. "Outward and — she pointed through the forest to where a huge, spreading tree towered above them all — magenward."

"I see," said Cara, although she didn't.

"Fancy being out in the forest during the float," the woman said to her kids, already turning away.

"Can she come with us, mama? She's got funny ears."

The woman turned around again, one hand on her hip. This was probably her best chance to find shelter. Cara put on her best 'welcome to the library' face that usually worked with anyone from kids to first timers.

"I'd be so grateful."

The woman paused. "I doubt you'd survive, otherwise."

Chapter 2

Cara

Cara walked through the village behind the woman and her family, trying not to make a squelching noise with her wellies. The woman had finally admitted that she had an inn, where Cara could come in and warm up. Ynore, that was the woman's name. A strange name, but beautiful in its own way.

The village, which was one main street lined with small thatched-roof cottages covered in flowering vines, had a hushed feeling. A sign that said 'Bracken' swung slightly in the breeze. Chickens pecked around in the grass, and a goose lifted up its head, and fixed its beady eye on her. Cara kept her gaze straight ahead at the dark purple material swishing around Ynore's legs, and decided that it was a cloak with huge sleeves. That would be useful as the sun had disappeared and the cold seemed to chill her skin wherever it touched. The children had run far ahead.

Back in Ledstow, Cara walked tall, knowing she was powerful. As one of the main coven who helped to protect the residents of the town, she was treated with respect. Here, no one looked twice at her. They could be peeking from their windows, she thought, with a shiver. Was that the twitch of a curtain?

The inn was just like the other houses, although twice as tall, and built around the trunk of one of the huge trees. A vegetable garden, that might once have been thriving and was now barely surviving, was spread around the side of the wall.

"Come in," Ynore said, looking out the heavy door before she shut it. "You can get an evening meal a bit later. I've got a room available that I can let you have to warm up."

Cara nodded gratefully. "I will repay you," she said. "Dishes or sweeping the floor. Whatever you need."

Ynore made a hmph sound.

"Can she play with us first?" the girl said, and what looked like a sea urchin spun through the air with a high whistling sound.

Cara caught it. It was knobbled but strangely smooth and with a decent weight.

"I suppose so," Ynore grumbled, heading behind the bar to get a flagon off the hook. "As long as you've fed the chickens."

"It's a nottle," the girl said and put her hands up, ready to catch.

"I'll be the naiad in the river," the boy shouted, which must be a variant of 'piggy in the middle'.

"Outside, then."

Cara followed them out the back. So far, things weren't too different.

LATER, CARA LAY IN her room, halfway up the tree, looking out at the leaves rustling through the window. Her stomach gave a long, low rumble. The fairy stories, myths and legends she had read streamed through her mind. What was she supposed to do if she couldn't eat the food offered to her? She checked her pockets for a chocolate bar or heck, she'd even settle for a stale cracker at this point. But they were empty, except for a bit of lint.

The room itself was gorgeous. She ran her hands over the curved wood of the wall, marvelling at the workmanship. The planks fitted together with no visible seam, like silk under her fingers.

She stepped onto a flat balcony fashioned from a branch. The village below was still, except for some chickens. A few blossoms were falling from somewhere and settled on the wood beside her feet. In any other circumstances, this would be breathtakingly beautiful. A drumming sound came to her, and she thought the children must be playing somewhere around the tree.

Back inside, she held her palms out and felt her magic building. The people here didn't know that she was powerful. They thought she was a weak human. But she still had her magic.

Witchcraft soothed her soul; a set of words to keep her safe, a selection of ingredients to ward off ill luck, rhythmic sweeping with her broom to get rid of the energy of the old year and welcome the new. It was as much a part of her as her love of books.

The drumming came closer and she went over to the window. She froze. The noise was the whirring of wings, as a dozen winged men appeared in the sky from behind. She leaned out to see. That must be what 'Magenward' was all about. A huge tree, much taller than the others, with branches that crossed over each other in a complicated pattern, spread wide far above her.

In an instant, a knock came at her door. She had taken two steps when the door swung inwards. Another heartbeat and a man appeared in her doorway, bending his head to get through. He was wearing what appeared to be a silver uniform and had very dark hair, pulled back in a half ponytail. He looked as if he was chiselled from stone and radiated power.

"Your name, please?" He eyed her as if she was a wild animal he wanted to cage.

Cara stepped back and pulled her cardigan around her. There was no way she'd be giving that out. "That woman said I'd be safe here."

"I said you could come in and get warm," came Ynore's voice from the stairwell. "You've done that."

"You lied." Cara spoke quietly, but her power built up as the betrayal burned inside. She lifted her hands, ready to cast a protection charm. It seemed as if she could trust no one here. But the man wiped his palm across, as casually as if he was wiping a mark off a cupboard door, and her magic fizzled and froze in her veins.

"We cannot lie," he said, casually. "We are not like mortals. Now don't get yourself in any more trouble."

The man gestured to walk onto the balcony. There was nothing for it. She looked over the edge, tempted for a moment to jump. But it seemed that he knew what she was going to do almost before she even thought about it. The height made her unsteady and she reeled back into a pair of strong hands that clasped her upper arms. A pair of velvet purple wings slowly unfolded above her and the arm went around her waist, gripping her tight.

Her feet lifted from the wood as she floated through the air, gaining height with each powerful flap of the wings. The others all rose up behind them. One solitary purple boot slipped off her stockinged foot and disappeared into the green canopy. All coherent thought slipped from her mind along with it, replaced by internal screaming, as she dangled in the air, far above the treetops.

"QUEEN TALYNN, FIRST Child of the esteemed Queen Argonne, Protector of the Realm, Holder of the Magen, Revered Wisdom of the Vernal Court and the Growing Chapel of Epicotia." A short man with long goat-like horns, in the same uniform as the other guard, gave the introduction.

The queen stood up from her petal throne and arranged her huge, bright pink dress around her, as if she had all the time in the world. It must have been at least an hour of waiting before even a word was spoken. Cara supposed the queen could take her time, but her own stomach was starting a protest that wouldn't be silenced. She willed herself not to look at the table covered in food that was opposite her.

She had already studied everyone in the hall; faerie people with skin from the darkest brown to the palest white, and even a man with greenish skin, whose face somehow reminded her of the pointy petals of an aquilegia. She tried to work out what everyone was there for and what the rules were here. If only she had an etiquette guide, or a reference book. Finally, it seemed that it was time for something to happen.

"On this day, The First, Prince Alawynn will hold court," the queen announced in a strong and low voice. "My time in active duties will soon run out and he is the next in line, as you know. Show him the same respect as you would afford me."

Cara's guard was sitting rigid next to her but he mumbled angrily every now and then. What was making him so grumpy? Surely, his job was to do what the royals said.

She had been too afraid to struggle much when she was dangling in mid air, instead thinking back to the self defence class she had taken once, preparing for when they landed. Get them off guard. Avoid the strike.

As soon as their feet were on land, she had bunched her hand into a tight fist, pulled back and hit him in the nose.

Oh, goddess, that hurt! As his hands came up, she stepped forward to knee him right in the soft bits—but he blocked her with his own leg. His fist came around her wrist and he twisted it behind her back and pushed her gently to turn around. She stumbled.

"Just play the game and you've got a chance for mercy, you silly mortal," he'd growled in her ear.

"Let go," she squeaked and he loosened his grip. Plants growing in the path made her look down so she didn't trip. "You talk about mercy," she said. "But you didn't even let me say anything."

He had simply glared at her, a trickle of blood running from one nostril and a dark line on his top lip. Much as he was glaring at the prince now.

Cara ran her fingers lightly over the knuckles of her right hand. She'd been lucky to catch him off guard and it likely wouldn't happen again.

"That's not good," the man muttered, sitting straight in his chair. He leaned across to her and whispered, "Do not annoy him. He is extremely quick to anger. Take it from me."

"Annoy him?" If she knew how to avoid offending anyone, but especially the royal family, that would be a great start.

She glanced over at her guard, who was breathtakingly handsome. He reminded her of a leopard. He had laid a short sword and a quiver of arrows on the seat between them but she was sure he could have a knife to her throat before she could say anything remotely annoying.

"Welcome to court. Please ensure you all speak clearly for the scribe," the guard who had announced the queen said, in his surprisingly rich voice. Cara had the absurd thought that he'd make a good radio DJ or YouTube influencer, before noticing that there was a shuffling around the room. "We will now question the strangers."

The prince, who had dark auburn hair pulled back in the same style as the guard next to her, got up from his seat at the side and strode towards the front. He stopped before the throne and bowed his head to the queen, then sat in the chair to the right. His head came up to the queen's shoulder height. It all seemed to be calculated. The queen put her hand out and three servants ran to her, their heads bent as they listened to some whispered command.

"Stand, stranger," Prince Alawynn commanded. "What were you doing in our lands?"

That's me, Cara thought, with a start. She stood and brushed her hands on her jeans.

"I came through here by accident," she said in the loud voice she used when reading a story to the children at the library. "Lost my way."

"She lies," stated one of the queen's ladies, who had long, red hair, and moved as if she was walking through water. Her voice was lazy too, as if she didn't care much about what she was saying. But the queen threw a glance her way.

"Thank you, Tuel." The Prince looked around at the crowd, his arms spread wide, as if there was an inside joke. "Do not speak any more untruths in this court. Show respect for the Crown."

"I was looking for my sister," Cara said, tightly.

"If you were indeed looking for your sister, describe the sister." Alawynn reached over and plucked a grape from a bunch on the table.

"Pale. Thin. Blonde hair. Otherwise, you know, like me." Normal height. No pointed ears, she thought. Not built like a Greek deity.

Prince Alawynn exchanged a significant look with the queen, who rearranged her rose skirts fastidiously. It seemed there was a silent battle of wills going on between them. After a moment, the queen spoke.

"We have seen this sister," she stated, sending a chill down Cara's spine as their eyes met. "Yes. It was twelve nights ago. We were dancing the new year in, when the birds began to speak."

Cara let out a giggle, from nervousness as much as the mental picture of them all dancing, and the Queen threw a look at her which froze the laugh on her lips. But they couldn't have really seen Serena, could they? It was only this morning that she'd gone missing, after all.

"Why do you bother telling her about it, mother?" The prince asked. "She's too ignorant. These mortals don't understand our ways."

Someone murmured in agreement.

"This is extremely serious for us," the queen continued, in the smooth voice of one who commands attention. "It means some creature has made a wish, and we must work as hard as we can to make it happen. Not because we have any obligation to do so, but because the creature has made a sacrifice."

The faerie court all turned to look at Cara. The weight of thirty dark eyes pressed on her back. She thought the guard next to her groaned softly.

"Oh, you mean me? I didn't make a sacrifice." Like a deer in the woods? She'd never slaughtered something in her life. "Can you let me speak?"

A gasp. Some shuffling.

"Take her to the holding rooms."

Two guards trotted up the aisles and once again she was lifted up and floated through the air.

She closed her eyes tight and it felt for all the world like she was inching upwards to the sickening top of a rollercoaster.

Chapter 3

Aeban

His first mistake. Aeban cleared the guard to land with a raised fist and realised, too late, from the crunch and squish underfoot, that it was on the edge of a patch of crops. He rubbed his boot along the grass.

The ground felt so *heavy*. He signalled to the others to wait and tapped lightly on the door. Ynore se Haira opened it immediately, her face creased in worry, and led the way upstairs. Perhaps she was too distracted to notice the garden.

He took the steps two at a time and reached for the door but a cold hand stopped him.

"Be gentle on her, aye?" Ynore asked.

"We'll do as we always do," he answered. "You know that. And you'll get your magen rebate."

"It's hard times," she said, quickly. "Hard times in the villages. We're not getting many guests here because of the new policy."

"I know."

"And will you replace those pumpkins? We can't grow them as easily out here."

"I'll send a messenger," he said. Of course she had noticed the squashed garden.

He pushed the door open slowly and paused in the doorway.

The first thing he saw was a woman with her arms raised as if to attack. She reminded him of a goddess, like Feisia who walked among the villagers. Her power radiated from her like the sun behind the clouds. He tried not to step back, not to show weakness. For all he knew, she was a descendant of the goddess come to test him. He questioned her but she didn't give anything away.

Almost without thinking, he drew on his power to make sure she had none.

The woman flushed in anger, but didn't move to draw any further weapon. He licked his lips. There was nothing for it. All strangers were to be taken magenwards, immediately. Humans were to be treated like any other enemy. He picked her up and got off the ground and felt the wind currents gather around him as he rose. The others followed.

In the air, he surveyed the land below, looking for anything out of the ordinary. A troop of feathered selmadores were on the move, sliding between stands of trees. The woman was still, at least.

The drawbridge was down so he landed on the planks, planning to run over their customs with the woman before she entered the court. Perhaps he could keep her out of too much trouble.

She was a witch, that much was clear. But he'd cut off her magical powers for now.

Fury radiated from every inch of her short frame, which he let his eyes roam over. From her one silly purple rubber boot, up her legs, hips and full breasts. Shit! He put one hand to his face as pain bloomed there. She'd hit him in the nose and her knee was precariously close to his—

He blocked, grabbed her hand and twisted it behind her, easily, ignoring the burning in his nose and lip. Hitting the captain of the guard! Most of the human prisoners couldn't fight much at all. He loosened his grip on her as it became obvious that she wasn't fighting anymore.

Obviously, his second mistake was underestimating her. He gave her a warning, then he crossed the bridge, chuckling to himself. It was fair enough on her part. If she didn't come from a warring nation, he could see how it might seem like overkill to take her to court straight away. But you couldn't be too careful about spying eyes. He glanced over her clothing, checking for any signs of Vulcairn stitching. It would be smart of them to send a human into their realm.

The court was quiet. Alawynn looked smug as a cat with cream up the front. Aeban almost walked back out as he realised he must look like he was straight out of a battle, covered in blood and with mud-spattered clothes from that wretched garden. The queen smiled over at him.

The ambassadors from two of their allied lands were sitting up the front. Lord Azul, stroking his wolf-fur stole and staring at the queen. Was he even drooling over her? To his left was Lady Dreia de Maine from the naiad lands. He wondered what it cost her to be away from home.

He bade the stranger to sit down and be still. He managed to sit through the formalities, giving tips to her when he could. But his knuckles whitened on the handle of his short sword when he realised that Alawynn was in charge today. Burn it, he'd forgotten.

She flushed when they spoke to her, a rose blush that spread over her neck, cheeks and the tip of her nose. He couldn't help but flinch when she stood up and answered the queen as if she was speaking to a street merchant. Everything, tone of voice included, had to be most carefully moderated. Everywhere in the realm, but especially in the court. Always. It was all a giant show, he thought, bitterly.

It was no surprise to him when it ended in the witch being sent up the tree. He watched her being floated out of the court, breathing through his nose. Another mortal who wouldn't listen.

"Come here," the queen called, after most of the officials had left. "What have you done to yourself?" She lifted her hand, a finger slid over the bridge of his nose and the familiar warmth knitted into his skin as it healed.

"Naught."

"There. That should do it."

"Probably wasn't paying attention during drills," Alawynn put in.

Aeban turned to leave, not in the mood for the jabs.

"Did you get flattened by one of your platoons, eh?"

"And you, Alawynn, must always address me as Your Majesty. Our primary relationship must be Crown and successor, now."

"It's only appropriate," Garin, the Herald, said from somewhere behind him. Aeban could imagine the stubborn little man ducking his head to avoid Alawynn's glare. He smiled to himself.

Food and drink would be welcome. He went to his chamber to find his cloak and headed for the tavern, tramping along the main cobbled street through the city. A few horses were tied up outside the buildings, flicking their ears to keep away the flying insects in the gathering dusk.

He had always loved dusk in the queendom; the rose red light cooling to purples and blues, as the float started. Petals wiggled loose from twigs and glided across the breeze to twirl and settle on the ground. It brought everything into focus. The court was not his whole life. He could escape from it for a while.

'Fight by day, float by dark' was a common saying. It was their way of life, a warrior's way of life. Aeban had learned to fight at six years old with his father's bow and arrow. Hand to hand, as well. Fighting his brother and their cousins. It was always the five of them until they joined the guard, practising the movements slowly at first, then gradually faster, until it was easy as scratching your nose. He feinted out of the way on a breath in, pulled the arrow from the sheaf on a breath out and loosed the arrow. And looked to the left to see that they had all done the same.

In the guard, no one was left behind. They marched together, flew in formation exactly two wingspans apart and landed in unison as much as possible. He was under no illusions that it was just for their safety, though. The members of the guard kept each other in line and would have no qualms about telling the higher ups if he did anything.

Thank Lumbris they didn't know what he was thinking, at least.

His mind wandered to the prisoners up the tree. There were far too many for his liking. They fascinated him with their lives like the blink of an eye and their impossible wishes. First of all, he'd wanted to know more about them so that he could accurately describe them for the histories. What did they think about? What motivated them? How could such a short life leave a legacy? How could any one of them make any difference among such a sea of people? Then he'd gone from watching them to talking to them.

He'd have to keep his eye on that new brown-haired witch. Anyone could see she wouldn't be leaving any time soon. She was far too opinionated and rude to abide by their customs. It was frankly embarrassing. The others might not be as kind as him.

The warmth of the tavern hit him as he pulled open the heavy door. The tavern was the best place to find out the mood of the people, something he felt was important as head of the guard. He threw a coin down on the bar and ordered a chestnut stew from Diggins, who greeted him with an ironic salute. He returned it with a grin and a rude gesture and found a table in a corner at the back. He pulled up his hood in spite of the heat, so he would be left alone.

The bard wore a large, floppy hat and plucked at his harp in the corner with long, clawed nails. He was singing one of the common ballads that had become popular in the last few years.

"Hear tell of trees in flame, hear tell

Through whispered words and tolling bells

That soon the towers crumble down

In the time of the dragonelle"

Two bearded men were drinking at a table and the bard was flirting outrageously with them, wiggling his hips. A man and woman were snuggling in a booth, their heads close together. Good, he thought. There was no one he knew here. He could settle into his meal and watch from the corner in blessed peace.

Gwyneth found him before he'd finished two spoons of the thick stew. She slid into the seat opposite and flicked her long, blonde braid over her shoulder.

"I thought I might find you here."

He let out a breath. "It's not often you show your face up above," he said.

The scribe passed a hand over her eyes. "Fennen was inscribing for the court today so I could get out. And it's difficult for most of us to mingle with the folk up here. Our thoughts cross theirs like a bridge curving over a road."

That was an understatement. "I know, Gwyn. So what are you doing?" A commotion near the bar caught his eye. The barkeep had come back from out the back to find one of the punters with one leg over the bar. Aeban watched to see if he might need to get involved.

"I was actually looking for you."

He rested his spoon in the bowl. "Why?"

"Well, it started when—" She shook her head and placed her hands on the table. "No, there's too much. I'm going to keep it brief. A rumble began and grew to a terrible growling. We took cover, thinking the earth was going to move. But it was *the turning*. You know what I mean. An unbearable few moments of grinding noise then a great silence."

He looked at her sharply. "Did it move much?"

"What was eastward moved to the west. So yes." She turned to look behind her as the barkeep was headed for them. "I know we don't know much about it all but... I'm very much afraid. Will you come? I didn't know who else to ask."

"Yes, I'll come."

She was gone, quick as the wind, and Diggins stood by the table, in her place, rapping his knuckles on the wood. The innkeeper had the large nose and forehead of a gnome and the body of a centaur. Aeban had known him a long time.

"Can I get you a flagon of moondew on this lovely evening? Just three silvers for a child of Randolynn. It would go down nicely after your meal. And one for the lady?"

"That is indeed a bargain," he said. "But I'll not partake tonight. The lady won't be coming back and it sounds as if I'll need my wits about me tomorrow." He lifted the bowl and drained the rest of the stew, which was warming, if not life-changing.

"We all need our wits about us," Diggins said, drily, casting a look over at the two men who had started a drunken jig, tossing the bard's hat between them. He grabbed the bowl as soon as it hit the table. "But we dance while we can."

Chapter 4

Cara

A dirt floor. That was the first thing that registered when she awoke. The smell of the earth beneath her face. The growling of her stomach had become a small animal that gnawed at her insides, pawing and biting for attention. How much time had passed?

She scrambled up onto her elbows and peered around. Above her, thick silver branches twisted around each other, crowded close so that only very small gaps remained. A grating could be heard from somewhere in the gloom. Scrambling along on her hands and knees, she checked the strength of the branches but they were strong and immovable. She scratched at the packed earth floor, experimentally, noting it would probably be easy enough to dig her way out if that became necessary.

She lay down, and looked for the magic in her veins, waiting for it to build and fill her with power. But what had been a constant source of strength for her for the last twenty years was no longer there.

"Of course not," she whispered. Tiredness overcame her and she huddled against the branch wall. At least it wasn't too cold.

Alright. What would Nynaeve do? Or Claire Fraser? They'd work out what they had in their arsenal, she thought with a snigger. Tools? None. Weapons? Only her body. She'd landed a hit on the guard when he was caught unaware. That wouldn't likely happen again. Allies?

"Hello?" She called, in a small voice that spun thinly out into the darkness. "Bonjour. Ola. Konnichi wa."

The scratching stopped. A hacking noise burst into the quiet.

"A new... friend," a raspy voice said. It sounded like a man. "Sorry, you'll.... have to be patient. It's been a while since I've talked to someone. English?"

"Yes. Hello," she said, feeling absurd, but not wanting to let the disembodied voice go. "Where are we?"

"Very high up the big tree. Holding cells for mortals. I've been in here a long time, let me see, for... 951 days, it must be."

"That's horrible," Cara whispered to him. "What did you do?"

"Well, it turns out I did something terrible in terms of faerie law. But I had no idea at the time." He coughed again. "It was a summer evening in July. I was getting ready to go down to the pub when I got the call. My wife, Jane, was in a car accident." His voice broke, and he was quiet for a moment. When he spoke again, his voice was low and soft. "She was in the hospital, in an induced coma. I wished, to anyone that would listen, for my wife not to die. I remember asking right there in that bare hospital room. Saying I would give anything. It came through really strong as it was on Beltane. That's what they told me."

"You would have given anything?" she asked. A sacrifice.

"Yes, and I have given up everything, haven't I? I don't even know if she is alive. If it worked."

Cara told him about the silly wishes they had made on Halloween night. "It all feels ridiculous now," she said. "I'm a witch but I don't usually dabble in wish magic. I was always told it was notoriously unreliable. Are you magical too? I guess you must be."

"I never thought so. My grandfather used to tell stories of his sister, whose dreams sometimes came true. I've had a lot of time to think about it, now. Perhaps I'm from a family of clairvoyants, but I always denied it. Well, more like I didn't really think of it. I was an insurance assessor, and I sometimes had visions of my clients leaving the oven on. The wife said I just thought about my work too much."

"So you knew about it before they made a claim?"

"I sometimes dreamt about it, yeah. Sounds a bit out there, doesn't it? The name's Nate Rosewood, by the way."

"Nate. I like it." Cara leant her face against the rough branch. A strong name, a friendly name. "I think you saved her, Nate."

"You ever been fishing? The way I figure it is that most wishes do absolutely nothing. They fizzle out like a dad joke at the dining table, right? Those are your fishes, slippery little blighters. But every now and then, one gets hooked by this world due to some set of circumstances and the faerie people reel it in and grant it. What did you do? For a job?"

"I was a librarian. I mean, I still am. I think. Love my job."

"I grew turnips." Nate stopped and cleared his throat. "At home. And spuds. They were quite big. No one cares about turnips these days, but I swapped them with the neighbours sometimes. I'd get beans, cauliflower and sometimes fresh peas from them in return. And Jane would add them to a soup, of course."

As Nate prattled on about his life, Cara reflected on how welcome it was to have someone with you when you were lost. Even an insurance assessor who liked turnips.

"Whereabouts did you live?"

"Oh. Leeds," he said. "Think my voice has had enough now." He collapsed into a coughing fit.

"It's lovely to meet you. Despite the circumstances." It seemed like he was sick and needed healing. Were the people here that uncaring that they wouldn't heal a sick human? She decided she'd give them the benefit of the doubt. Perhaps they didn't know how to heal humans.

"You don't sound as upset... as folks usually are," he noted. His voice was curious.

"I don't see the point. It takes a lot to upset me." She lay back and curled her hands into fists. But if you mess with my sister, I'll swerve straight past 'upset', pedal to the metal, for 'revenge', she thought.

"Goodnight, new friend."

Through the cracks above her, she could see a diamond-shaped light, velvet sky and bright stars overhead. It could easily have been her own world if she stared at that one little patch of sky.

"We're going to get out of here, Nate. I promise."

In response, there came a faint wheezing that could have been a laugh.

BY THE NEXT DAY, CARA'S stomach had become a yawning void. From the books she'd read, she knew what accepting food here did to mortals. But she had no choice. She had to eat. If food was offered to her, she'd take just a little bite. Enough to survive. A little bite wouldn't do anything to her, surely.

She knelt beside the wall and began scraping at the earth. It was soothing work and, most of all, it felt like she was doing something to take control.

A creaking noise became a grinding and the twigs rustled their leaves, then the branches began moving apart. Sunshine poured in through the gap, making her turn away.

When she opened her eyes, a man was standing there. The guard from yesterday was wearing soft silver clothes that clung to his body on the top half and billowed out gently around his legs. He brushed his long dark hair behind his ear, which was pointed at the top. His nose was straight and perfect and his lip complete, with no sign of any cut, almost as if she hadn't struck him yesterday.

"Did you get into any trouble overnight?" His lips curled upwards slightly in the ghost of a smile.

She stood up. "Are you letting me out?" She wiped her hands on her pants, unobtrusively, to get rid of any telltale dirt.

The man shook his head. "No, I'm not. However, I do apologise sincerely for the accommodations. During the day, we allow you access to everything we have, including the courtyard and the contemplation pool. I'm sure you'll find it satisfactory. We provide a pail of water for cleaning your hands and face."

Satisfactory? Was this guy for real?

Cara scrambled towards the door and looked around in wonder. If this was a prison, what was the rest of the realm like? The floor opened out to a huge area with small clearings surrounded in branches, like her own, around the edge. People were slowly emerging, stretching and blinking in the light. The courtyard was surrounded by huge walls, covered in vines and flowers, alive with the humming of bees. There looked to be garden patches in the middle. At the far end was a tall domed structure with climbing plants trailing up it.

He showed her the pool, which swirled of its own accord, begging her to stare into its depths. To her left was a long table filled with all sorts of fruits of bright green, yellow and purple. Vegetables, nuts and green stems covered in grapes filled in the gaps. She licked her lips.

"Eat. Please," he said, seeing where she was looking. "Help yourself."

With dread in her heart, she tried to stop. But somehow her feet ended up next to the edge of the table and her fingers filled with berries, almost before she realized. The juice ran sweet and tart across her tongue, as she ate as many as she could. The peach she bit into was somehow sweeter and fresher than any she'd ever tasted.

The man watched her with an amused smile. So much for keeping away from the food.

"Come on," he said, finally, looking towards the other end of the space. "There is much more where that came from."

She looked up at him. "Are you going to let me speak today, then?"

He inclined his head a little but waited, in silence, for her to lead the way.

At the very end of the courtyard, she stepped into a room that was at once familiar and strange. The scent gave her a sharp stab of homesickness. It was a library, she was sure, from the welcoming sweet paper smell. Cara ran her fingers along the spines. Around the walls were lecterns with open books propped up in them, the pages slowly flicking over, as if tickled by a breeze. A wooden chaise longue window seat covered in embroidered cushions invited her to sit down.

"You're welcome to read our histories," the guard said.

Drinking it in, she addressed him quietly. "If what I have done is so bad, why are they keeping me alive? I mean, why here? Why not banish me back to — back home?" Her voice came out wobbly on the last word and she took a deep breath.

"This tree is larger than you could imagine and it expands to fit all of our allies down the bottom and all of our enemies near the top. There is plenty of room for everyone."

"All of the prisoners?" she asked. How many were there?

"Yes," he said. "I am named Aeban se Randolynn. How might I address you?"

Her name came into her mind. An amulet. She hoped she wouldn't forget it while she was here. But she was not going to offer it up to this oddly formal creature who was once more trying to find out her name. "I'm a librarian. If anyone knows the power of words, it is me. I will not be giving you my name."

He bowed his head in acknowledgement. "Then I'll call you Cunning Woman, for that's what you are, isn't it?" He smiled this time. "A witch?"

She shook her head. "No, I don't like that," she said, and she thought of the heavy books of fairy tales she had read, bright pictures gilt with gold. Let's turn this fairy story on its head, she thought. "How about Charming?"

"Whatever you prefer." His voice had a rich quality that made her want to hear him speak again but he seemed to be a man of few words, as he lapsed into silence, watching her.

"Your nose healed quickly," she said, showing him her knuckles, which were dotted with blood.

He frowned. "I asked the queen to heal it. But I'd really rather not have to do that again, if you don't mind."

"Let me guess. You were just doing your job?"

He nodded, eyeing her from his spot beside the door.

"I've read many stories of people making poor choices while 'doing their job,'" she murmured, her hands already reaching out to caress the leather-covered books in the shelf closest to her. A History of Prophesy and Scrying. "Sometimes you have to question things. Perhaps talk to people first?"

"I do talk." He waved away her comments. "Well, I can see you want to explore the tomes. I'll leave you to it."

"Just a little bit," she said. "Unless the alternative is getting out of here?"

"I'll return later with a healer," he said and was gone in an instant.

HE WAS TRUE TO HIS word and returned that evening as the shadows were lengthening along the floor of the library.

Cara was absorbed in looking at a scroll which had a beautiful map of the villages; Willowville, Nut Hill and Bracken, painted in what looked like shining watercolours. But what caught her eye was the city, Epicotia. It was painted to be very large, with tall towers. It could be artistic license, of course. She looked up to find him standing just inside the door.

"What are you doing?" he asked, eyeing the books and scrolls that surrounded her on the floor.

"Oh, well, I noticed that there were a few books about the Mortal Realm. So I thought they should all go together. Then I found some about Creatures of the Lake and they were mixed in with histories of the villages—"

"You were rearranging the bookshelves?" He quirked an eyebrow.

"I might have been." She began closing the books and piling them into something resembling tidy. Books needed to be stored in a system. People needed to be able to find exactly what they needed.

Aeban opened his hand to reveal a small bottle. "I've brought something to help."

She looked up. "Oh! I was a little worried that you were going to bring the queen here. You said she healed your nose."

He grunted. "No, she wouldn't come this far up. The healer was busy but he sent this salve. He said to apply it to the grazed skin. And it might cause some numbness."

He put his hand out for her to lay hers on top.

She crossed her arms, looking up at him. "Thanks. I can handle a graze. What I can't handle is being stuck in here when I need to find my sister." She wasn't going to be fed, watered and healed by these cruel people. What would they take in return?

"Just give me your hand."

After a long moment where he regarded her with a flat stare and she flashed her eyes, defiantly, she gave in with a sigh. She placed her hand in his, feeling absurdly like some Regency lady about to take a turn around the garden. He spread it over her knuckles, taking time to make sure it was all rubbed in.

She had to admit that, after an initial freezing feeling, it soothed the sting. "Thank you. Um, how come this picture is almost entirely of the city?" she asked, to avoid his dark silver eyes that were burning into her. He was very close.

"That's what the artist wanted to portray," he said, cryptically.

Cara was even more confused than ever. She'd seen, when they were flying in, the relative size of the city to the villages. It wasn't that much bigger. Unless, perhaps, it used to be much larger?

His answers were unsatisfactory, that was for certain. But she could definitely make use of the fact that he could only tell the truth. She needed all the information she could get if she was to get out of here with her sister.

She didn't want to look at him, to show him that she needed his help. But, just for an instant, she met his gaze. His eyes burned with an intensity she wasn't expecting. He had a slight scar next to his mouth that moved when he smirked.

She lifted her chin. "How long am I supposed to stay here?"

"It's entirely at the whim of the crown. Oh, and don't think of trying to escape. The walls are covered with a plant that has a certain hooked thorn, that I'm told is unspeakably painful, and the bees are also trained to swarm."

Chapter 5

Aeban

Aeban shook hands with Gedre as he landed. He liked to make sure he was there for at least the first rounds of the morning. Perhaps it made a difference to the prisoners to have someone polite to greet them each day.

"Good morrow, brother." Gedre was a dryad who had low vision, since he'd been hit by an incurable mud curse. But his other senses seemed to be keen, if not sharpened. He walked straight over to the closest cell and moved the branches open.

Aeban headed towards the cell on his left. Seeing the prisoner again, kneeling on the floor of the den, one hand raised against the light, he felt off kilter once more, as if she was a threat. He moved into a defensive stance before checking himself. The human witch couldn't be any danger to him. It didn't make sense. She was weaponless, powerless and locked up. She was a creature tethered to the ground and couldn't even fly.

But the cold sweat on his forehead suggested otherwise. He hadn't even drunk moondew last night. What was he thinking?

In the guard, a mistake meant that someone got hurt, didn't eat or wasn't prepared. A mistake meant flying into a whirlwind spell or hailstrike. Errors meant good people might not come back.

He prided himself on becoming captain of the guard on his own merits and learning everything he could about his people; their likes and dislikes, their loved ones, what they valued and what they despised.

While their complaints were sometimes hard to hear, it helped him put the right people in the right places.

His work at the prison was no different. He showed the human witch around, watching her reactions carefully.

"How did you get here?" he asked, while she was leaning over looking at the contemplation pool. "Into the realm."

"I'm not exactly sure, but I think I fell through some sort of invisible... door. There were wild flowers and toadstools."

He nodded. "What you couldn't see was likely a portal. Where, may I ask, did you arrive?"

"It was next to a lake in the Auld Forest."

He looked up sharply. "Is that the truth? You shouldn't have been able to come through there."

"What do you mean? I don't lie all the time, like you seem to think I do. Of course that was where I arrived. There was a really bright lake, surrounded by trees, and a hill with castle ruins on top in the distance."

Heat ran through him at her tone. She obviously underestimated them all, from her rude questioning of a member of the royal family — in front of the entire court, no less.

The other thing about errors was that they often came in threes. Once you made one, your head was no longer in the game and it was all too easy to make more. Perhaps his third mistake was yesterday, thinking that he could do anything to help her.

"Why did you have to act like that?" he asked, anger flaring at her flagrant disregard for their customs. "In the court. I warned you that you must use respect. Why not make it easy on yourself?"

She didn't respond but he already knew why. It was evident in the easy way she spoke, the way she held her shoulders. Back home, she was powerful.

AEBAN STOPPED TO CHAT to another prisoner before he left but his thoughts were elsewhere. That woman was becoming a real burn in his side. He was getting used to that feeling of getting punched in the stomach every time he saw her. But if it wasn't a sign that she was a danger to him, what was it? Perhaps she was tied to his destiny in some way. He couldn't see how; she was easily subdued and her magic removed, so that she wasn't a threat. In his world, at least, and he didn't plan on going to hers any time soon.

He took flight for the destinarium, while the float was in full swing, blossoms twirling around him. He soared up through the pink, just to feel the wind currents gather under him, and looked back towards the kingdom. It saddened him to see it like this. Then he dove down through the branches, down down down to flit between the leaves, flying over singing and laughing voices, down past the ground.

There were still people down here, although far fewer than there had been when he was a child. Their voices were subdued, their faces drawn. He floated gently down and landed on the balcony of The Great Library.

At night, the creative mind came alive in the realm. The sculptors sculpted their clay into elegant statues and fountains. The ones who were proficient in green-casting grew new varieties of plants. The bards sang in their music chambers and in the taverns. Weavers wove, bakers of sweet treats concocted their delicacies. People debated for hours in high open balconies, flying off when they'd had enough. The scribes wrote the histories.

Aeban was lucky to be proficient in several disciplines. As one of the scribes, he was an inventor. They used magic to describe new objects in detail, which were then brought to life in the histories. Most of the scribes lived below, hardly visiting the upper city.

The outer door was locked but he spoke the words and it clicked open. He entered the moonlit entranceway and walked towards the lamplight, where a few scribes were working. How could he observe the ceiling without being seen? It would take at least a few hours of observation to clearly map it.

"Aeban," Gwyneth said, sidling up next to him when she spotted him. "Thank you for coming so quickly."

"I can't be seen to be looking up," he said. "But one glance tells me that it's very different."

"It has changed much," she replied, her face creased with worry. "Everyone else is pretending it never happened."

"Have you raised it with anyone?"

"When it first happened, a few of us mentioned it. But the rest steadfastly ignored it. We've had scrolls appearing on doors, reminding us not to be distracted by it."

"It's ridiculous," he said, passing a hand over his stubbled chin. "Can you do me a favour? Can you map the celestial bodies for me? Then I'll find a way to get them read. I think I'm being followed some of the time. And the network… "

Gwyn's eyes darted around the room. "It might take me a while. We're not meant to stargaze, so I'll have to take small glimpses at a time."

"Fine. That's fine. I know you can do it, Gwyn. Leave it in the 51st page of the fourth book in the Mycology shelf."

"Alright."

Something had caused a huge change in their fortunes. He only hoped it didn't mean a turning point in the war.

Chapter 6

Cara

Each morning, she asked her guard if she was getting out today. Calmly, of course. It would pay to keep him onside. She worked on her tunnel overnight, scraping at the floor. She ate the delicious food, chewed on the strange herbs that grew around the cells to clean her teeth, and drank nettle tea. She began tending the garden in the prison.

Small pleasures kept her alive. If having Nate next door to reminisce about their world was her sustenance, the library was her salve. Each day, she found a warm spot in the sun and read the histories. If she reached towards a page, it changed so that she could comprehend it. She learnt about the wonderful people that lived in this realm; the selkies and the sirens, the naiads and the dryads, and the many faerie families. The way the books were written was very poetic, almost as if they were stories made up to teach something, similar to fables in her world.

Her eyes flicked to the door, where Aeban stood, rocking lightly on his heels. He seemed to be constantly keeping an eye on her. He talked to some of the other prisoners each day but she was sure she wasn't imagining that he spent more time near her than the others. What was it about her that made him so worried?

The page flicked open to the exact place she had left it, yesterday, and Cara gaped in surprise. But after scanning the page, she frowned.

"Did that really happen?" she called to her guard. It was an offhand question, but she suddenly realized that he could be of help to her. She desperately needed information and he only spoke the truth.

"Our histories are based on real events, yes."

"But 'the skies turned dark as night when the tree rotted, and all seemed desolate'. That can't be right?"

He came a little closer to look at the page. "We cannot tell an untruth, remember, but some of our stories are... a little more figurative."

She raised her eyebrows. That sounded a lot like fiction books in her professional opinion. "Alright. What's that about then?"

"This speaks of the decade of the cave nymph, a time that brought famine to the kingdom as nothing would grow well. A horrible time when the gods left us."

"How did people get through it?"

"The royal family sent scouts to their allies. With all of their might combined, the land was slowly restored, magically. It took a long time but it strengthened ties with the other lands. So it's thought to be a good thing."

The talk of strengthening ties reminded her of Serena. Although Cara was not one to get overly upset, it felt ridiculously frivolous to sit in here reading when she could be finding her. Somehow, it felt as if her memories of home were sliding out of her mind. She would make sure she spoke of them with Nate again tonight.

"Will I get out of here?" she asked, abruptly. Heat flushed her cheeks. "How can you think it's alright to keep people here against their will? It's barbaric. My neighbour needs to be healed. I sleep on the hard ground. How many others here have never been given a second chance? For what, simply making a wish? We didn't know it would actually do anything."

His jaw tightened. "It is the way here." He slipped out the door, leaving Cara to her books.

AT NIGHT, SHE SPOKE through the wall with Nate; he told her about his favourite place to watch the football and the spot in his office where you could watch people feeding the ducks at the park. She told him about the usual library visitors, the shows she and Serena watched, and the members of her coven. The nightly ritual was an evocation of all the things they held dear, a way of keeping them alive. It was bright things to hold onto in the lonely strange nights.

One afternoon, she was reading about the Battles of the Naiads and spotted a tale that was written in strange, sloping writing.

When Aeban appeared at the door, she looked up. "What is this one about? It's written differently to the others."

"You've stumbled upon an old tale." He came up behind her. "You really are hungry for books, just like when you gobbled the food out there," he teased. "It speaks of the Rose flower and the Rosehip. They were joined together always, the best of friends. The Rose refers to the queen. The Rosehip was her sister, Margara. The queen has not spoken to her sister in many years."

His fingers slid over hers and she felt her heart start to race.

She cleared her throat. Concentrate, she told herself. But her hormones weren't that easy to convince. They were sassy little things that seemed to have had four wines and were irresistibly drawn to the dancefloor, shaking what their mama gave them. They didn't want to listen.

"Are they all in the same language?" she decided to ask, moving a step further away. "All of these books?"

"No, there are many languages for all of the creatures of the realm. But they are translated for everyone who reads them. I should know, I helped to write most of these."

"You did?" She'd met authors through her work at the library and always thought they were really dedicated, if a little weird. This was a man whose every lithe movement screamed warrior.

He nodded. "But don't look so affected. Writing the histories is not a well respected job in this realm. It used to be different." His hand wandered down the page. "This part speaks of manners. We have strict rules about how we speak to each other. And the further magenwards you live, the more respect you command. It is not respectful to answer someone directly, rather prefacing your speech with 'In my opinion' or 'It is thought that'. It is fascinating how you do not know any of these rules." His breath tickled her ear.

"What about this one?" She pointed to a scroll that was decorated in intricate patterns and bright colours.

"This is a re-telling of one of our most famous stories, The Chalice and the Stone. Randolynn was a brave warrior who—"

"That's your surname," she interrupted. "Randolynn."

"We each choose the most revered of our ancestors to name ourselves after. We use 'se' which means 'from the forest of'. So I'm Aeban se Randolynn." He waved his hand to dismiss the custom, but Cara thought that was a lovely convention. That way, you could choose who and what you valued and add it to your own name, as part of your identity. Who would she add to her own name? Serena, she thought.

"The thrust of the story is that Randolynn wanted to prove himself," Aeban continued. "He was a strong and skilled fighter in his own town but he travelled for many days and nights far away from his birthplace. He found some of the most fearsome beasts and became an expert warrior. But the further he went and the more enemies he slayed, the more washed out he felt, as if he was killing a little piece of himself each time. People that surrounded him looked up to him as a hero but he craved actual connection. He started to forget the way home. He lay down in a desert valley, the most forlorn and lonely place, determined not to go any further.

After three days, a fearsome beast appeared to him. In this version, it is a hydra. He could hardly summon the will to fight. But the hydra taunted him, saying it would find all of his loved ones. In Randolynn's foggy state, he could hardly remember them. But as the monster slashed at him and he walked towards the light, his mother's face came back to him. He stood, unsteady, and fought. It took him another two days until he slayed the beast.

When he did, it began to glow with a blinding light. The god Lumbris walked out of the beast's skin, smiling at him. You passed a great test, the god said. In return, he offered Randolynn three gifts. The first was The Stone, which is what you'd call a seed. It was given to him to be the home that he craved. The second was The Chalice, a small pot of concentrated magic. In this version, it was given to him to create exquisite beauty. The Stone split and sprouted and this is how we have the Great Tree, a place to house our people."

The tree she was in right now. "You said three gifts?"

"The other one was his soulmate."

Cara sighed. "That's lovely. So the tired and jaded warrior got a beautiful home and a family of his own, I'm guessing, since you're descended from him?"

Aeban nodded. "Yes, he started all of this."

His dark slate eyes bored into hers. They held passion, but also fear.

Cara held his gaze and he looked away first. *Why do you shy away?* She wondered. *What are you afraid of?*

SHE EMERGED FROM THE library into the courtyard to see people lounging on the long benches, chatting quietly. An old woman was standing by the pool, staring into its depths. A man came up beside her and bent down next to the water.

A young person was executing a complicated series of kicks, steps and punches over and over, their dyed blonde hair flipping as they moved. They couldn't be more than fifteen. What had these people done that was so bad?

Nothing, the answer came to her. They were simply desperate.

She found herself next to the pool, her eyes drawn by colours in the murky water. She shook her head and looked away.

Cara's eyes fell on one of the burrowed out spaces covered in thickly entwined branches that were used as cells. There appeared to be a face floating in the tree.

She walked closer, looking around her once to see if her guard was watching. He was talking to one of the prisoners. She bent low to get through the opening.

What on earth? A human with completely white hair cleared his throat once. Twice. She knew that sound well.

"Nate," she said, dropping down next to him. His face was perfect, but her eyes cast over his body, which seemed to be growing into the tree, sinews and bone blending seamlessly with the plants. "What? Why didn't you tell me?"

He opened his mouth and jiggled a branch that joined his lower lip to the tree.

"Figured you'd find out soon enough."

"We have to do something," she said. "We can pull you out," she finished, lamely.

He sighed.

"We can't let this happen," she said, again.

"It already has, my friend. I appreciate the concern but you need to worry about yourself."

"Goddess, Nate." She rubbed her forehead, as horror turned to despair. "What do you mean?"

"The pool."

"The pool?" She looked behind to where the woman was looking into the contemplation pond. She seemed happy and calm.

"It shows you all those you love the most, like a reality show. Alive or dead, they're in there. Whether you admit you love them or not. Whether you've lost touch with them or not. You can get obsessed with that stuff."

She glanced at the pool again and a shiver passed over her

shoulders. "Alright, I won't look into it."

"Hey, you might get a chance to get out. Make sure you show utmost respect to the queen. She has ultimate authority here. You might have to spend an entire day in the court. One wrong word from you and you'll be in here forever. And you can't trust any of them faerie people."

Cara thought of her hearing with the queen, and shame burned her cheeks when she remembered how she had let out a laugh about their customs.

"I doubt they'll ever give me another chance."

"Well, if you get another hearing in the court, do exactly what they say. Don't try to be clever. Always tell the truth. Take it from me. They will not show mercy."

Cara took the knowledge and held it, a small hard shell. It was the least she could do. For Nate, for all of them.

IN SPITE OF CARA'S best efforts to ignore him, she had to admit that the best way to learn about the realm was to hear from Aeban. Each day, he appeared at the door to her cell or in the library and, despite some initial reservation, he seemed willing to teach her.

He read to her most days, his long legs stretched out on a chaise, while she sat at the other end, listening to his musical voice recount feasts, factions, arguments, births and deaths, all in beautiful language that brought the birds, plants and creatures of the land to play, flourish and flutter at her feet. If it was another life, another place, this would be perfect.

"This story is about the twin archers. 'Born in pairs, always struggling,'" he said. "'Only one prevails'. This is a common saying about children."

"So twins are common here?" she asked. "Twins are quite rare back home."

"Whenever there is a birth among our people, there are always two infants," he replied.

"Every time?"

"Yes, but we are not blessed with children as often as humans. We would feel that Lumbris smiled on us if it was every hundred years."

"So have you got a lookalike somewhere, then? Well, at least you always have someone to hang around with. I always had my sister."

He frowned. "It's not that simple."

Before Cara realised what she'd done, she told him about her powers, what it was like to be part of a coven, and what her village, Ledstow, was like. She described all the staff at the library.

"I loved getting those twisty requests. Like we had a man come in who said he'd never read a book in his life but his neighbour told him he had to read 1984. So he came in and got it. Loved it, too. Oh, it's a novel about surveillance and censorship and... never mind. After that, he's come in a few more times looking for other books. A mother asked me to recommend a book for her child as the parents were getting separated. We have a Spanish family whose father came here. They thought they'd try and get books in Spanish for him. I ordered them through an interlibrary loan. The smile on his face was everything. He keeps on coming back to get more every month."

"You miss it," he said.

"Of course. I think that in my own small way, I was helping." She reached over and touched his hand, and asked him to help her escape. "My sister," she managed to say, around the lump in her throat. "She needs me."

He stamped his legs down to the ground, his gaze straight ahead.

"You cannot ask me that. I'm merely a younger son and that is, for all intents and purposes, equal to a commoner. That's why I'm in the guard. My brother already looks down on me because I come and spend time with the" — he looked away from her — "prisoners."

"Well, your brother's a fool," she joked.

In the silence, she watched his face. The dark brows drew together, and his face seemed to hide a storm of emotion.

"I have made a grave mistake being here," Aeban said. "I'll not come again." He stood up.

"Wait. Why?"

"My brother is The Crown Prince Alawynn, the heir to the throne. No one is to speak of him in that manner, not even lightly. I could…" His knuckles whitened on the wooden arm of the chaise but he didn't expand further on what punishment she had earned.

The heir to the throne. So she had not imagined the resemblance between them. Prince Alawynn was his brother. "Oh," she breathed. "Alright, I'm sorry. Please keep visiting me."

He stayed in the room, but Cara felt that the space between them had widened once more. She picked up a book and flicked through a few pages, idly.

"Hang on a minute. You said you're the younger son. But you told me the other day that everyone is born a twin here."

He grunted. "We decide things in our own way."

She looked at him, thoughtfully. For a race that prided themselves on the truth, they managed to confound with their words.

Chapter 7

Aeban

Night was the best time to visit. He quickly turned down a dim passage to the left, passing lamps that were out. Was no one even replacing them anymore?

Burn it, where was it? If he got to the old Department of Astrology, he'd gone too far. Right, here. He pulled the heavy door across and slid in through the gap.

The courtyard was silent, and just a sliver of moonlight trickled in through the cracks in the stone. He reached the other end in two strides and bent down. A great root of the tree lay exposed against this wall, gleaming silver-white.

He knelt for a long time, until his knees ached to take flight and his ears strained to hear the sounds of insects in the dirt. But she would wait longer, of course. His discomfort was nothing.

"Dearest Aunt," he said, surprised at the loudness of the words in this chamber, even though he whispered.

He waited for a slight creaking. His eyes flicked up to the branch that had grown from the great root, where something glinted. The branch, withered and old, had grown around a jewel. It was his aunt's bracelet and all that was left of her. She'd begged to keep it. He placed his hand lightly over the shiny black surface of the onyx.

"You should be glad in some small way that you can't see what has happened to us. It's not what your grandmother would have wanted, that's for certain. I've come here tonight because I'm asking for your help with the Seeing. I'm sorry I haven't learned the art. It's wartime still and I'm needed elsewhere. You're the only one who can read the fates, now."

"A stranger has come into our lands and I... have a feeling that she is important. A human witch, a librarian. Very powerful. She arrived on the fourth eve of summer and she's been imprisoned by the court."

There was a low groan.

"By the queen. Yes, well. You know her. This witch made a bargain, like so many of her kind do. Like you did, in the end. But I can't see that the fates want her to become part of *this*." He stopped for a moment, swallowed twice.

He tried to remember what Gwyneth had shown him so far.

"As far as I can see from the celestial bodies, Feisia is ascendant. Jupiter is in Bilious and there is a lot of movement in Potentia. And for some reason, the Archer cluster aligns with the Advocate. I think she's the Advocate. She has not completely finished mapping the whole thing."

The branch moved slightly toward his hand.

"Cursed flames," he said, softly, to the night sky. "If you can save someone else from the same fate as this, do it. We saw it coming the last time but we left it too late. I'm sorry for leaving it too late."

Silence. He hung his head.

If anyone knew he was here, they'd say he had his mind buried below ground, staring up at the fate maps. He was too compassionate for this world. After all, the trees who spread the most roots got the sunshine and water. He was a 'bleeding heart' in the guard who spent his free time with the prisoners. But he couldn't help caring about what happened to them. They were people, curse it.

He knelt for long moments, listening to the footsteps above. He thought of the people who still lived down here. He was about to get up, to move his aching legs. A creak. Were his joints creaking like a ship now? Was he that far into the twilit decades?

A creak. He held his breath. The branch moved, inch by inch, until it was pointing directly between his ribs.

IN THAT MOONLIT COURTYARD, a sliver of ice had chinked into the space where his heart should be. A frosty little certainty. There was no point arguing or questioning the fates. People could be bound to each others' fates in many ways. However, it was perfectly clear what his aunt wanted to say. The human witch was tied to his destiny.

Knowing that, though, didn't help much. In fact, it was a giant knot in the wood, he thought. He still wasn't sure how or why.

He tramped grimly towards where the others were waiting in the meeting house, a branched building inside a whisper tree that was supremely secure. No one outside could hear what was spoken inside. He thought that was one of the more inspired creations of his people.

"Brother," said Murrell, sitting shirtless on the edge of the table. "We've been waiting for you." Gnomes didn't feel the cold and, although they were au fait with the customs and manners of the faerie court, they also took off their clothes whenever they thought they could get away with it. Which happened to be quite often, given the circumstances.

"You don't have much choice," Aeban joked. "I'm leading the meeting."

His words fell into the silence like the heavy footfall of a human. The soldiers glanced at each other. It felt like he was missing something.

"What's up, *i harada*?" he asked, speaking casually to put them at ease, to remind them that he was one of them, that they had trained together since they were young.

"A message came through that we should be ready to have strategy training this week. It sounds like they want to pick someone else to lead the planning of the advance." Gorinn spoke casually, his huge hands wrapped around a flagon of something steaming hot. Nothing ever fazed him.

Curse her, Aeban thought, with a sigh, but he managed to smile to keep the others feeling comfortable. Let's keep them guessing about whether he knew of these developments.

"Well," he said through his teeth, "you've got me for now."

He leaned over, drawing a quick outline of the lands on the huge scroll that covered the table.

"How come you haven't done this already?" he asked Murrell.

The gnome shifted a little. "I'm sorry sir. I didn't know what the plan was going to be."

"Nothing's changed." Aeban pressed a little harder with the ink than he usually would and ripped the paper.

"Of course," Murrell said, though he raised his bushy eyebrows, that contrasted with his hairless chest and bald head.

"Right. We have the Vulcairn over here," Aeban said, then outlined a quick mountain and a few circles beneath it. "Closer than they have been since we can remember. We can't let them make any headway. That's the centre of gravity. Most of our troops are to the North. What news comes from the camp?"

He looked to Lord Azul and his Lieutenant, who were from the Wolflands. "A few small skirmishes but we think they're biding their time until they can amass the forces. Our troops have tried to engage but they are making sure we know it's going to be on their terms."

"That's not ideal."

"No," he said. "The troops up there are losing heart rapidly. It's a terrible place to make camp and the storms are getting more fierce. Perhaps if we sent some more of the fae guard up there to rally them?"

"It seems I can't spare any more." He couldn't say that it was because there weren't any more to send. Everything was about keeping up the appearance of strength. "You know that I would if I could, brother."

Lord Azul growled. "Armies need a reason. They won't keep going, otherwise. As you well know, Aeban se Randolynn. You used to be a great captain."

"And you used to be a young man."

"YOUR MAJESTY," HE SAID. "Father."

"Darling," his mother said, getting up from the seat by the windows, where she was being read to by one of her ladies. Tuel shook her red locks, folded her copy of the Bardian, got up and moved away to a respectful distance, although Aeban knew she would still be listening.

"How are you doing, son?" His father looked up. Menuel's once-dark hair and beard was now all silver. His face was youthful, although he was fifty years older than the queen and coming into the twilight of his life. His sharp features and warrior reflexes had softened, somehow, as he spent his days advising the different councils, but his eyes were still as acute as ever.

Aeban's mother regarded him from arm's length. "You've been drawing a little too much magic, I see. Have you also been drinking too much moondew?"

"I don't have time for that."

"Spending too much time away from the forest, then? Something concerns you."

Aeban stepped away from the scrutiny and took a seat opposite in the petal chair. These seats were comfortable and he stretched out, putting his hands behind his head.

"Your brother is looking really good," his mother continued. "He won the tournament last eve, which looks great for the crown. He's really stepping up."

"It looked serious for him for a while," his father said.

Aeban said nothing. Alawynn had always managed to win when it counted.

"Do you remember Veda's mother?" his mother asked, in an apparent change of topic.

"Yes, of course." Venera se Wemila was one of their army's best archers, with a wit to match. She had been a real asset in their march to Hektorel back in the time of the wasp.

"Then you'll know she was slain in the battle last week."

His heart clenched. "I did not." He paused, then murmured, "Even the mightiest tree."

"The Five protect her," his father replied, in the standard response. "And always revere her."

"The mourning continues," his mother said, with a sigh. "Day six so far. You should go and visit her," she added, lifting her eyebrows, always pushing him.

"Veda will have her close friends around her," he replied. "I came to talk to you about something," he said, leaning forward. "I really need you to consider sending some more of the guard up to the camp. At the very least, it would be prudent to send one or two sirens up there."

"You are well acquainted with how stubborn they are."

He wanted to say that they might be more accommodating if the queen hadn't blamed their king for her last poor decision, but he held his tongue.

"There is a prisoner. A human."

Talynn shook her head and reached for a cup that was on the table next to her. "You're not pleading the case for another prison rat?"

He made himself unclench his jaw. "She doesn't deserve to stay there."

"Sappy heart," his father said, although it was said with love.

His mother's voice was brisk, business-like. "Tell us about it."

"She's the witch who was looking for her sister. She made that wish not knowing what the consequences would be. I understand she's a much-needed member of society back in her homeland. All I'd ask for is a chance for her to be heard again. I'll teach her the proper manners and to treat us with respect. She wants to learn, I think."

"The wish was granted, though. We can't be seen to be going back on our bargains, son."

Aeban looked at his father.

"Ignorance is normally not an excuse, as you know," the queen said, lost in thought. "Well, it might actually work in our favour this time. We will agree to seeing her in court again, as long as you tell her how we expect her to behave. It might be good for the court to see one such as her subdued and respectful."

"You might have a point," his father agreed.

His mother savoured a mouthful of what he assumed was her favourite Epicot liqueur, eyes closed, before fixing him with a stare. "In return, you will defer to your brother for the strategy of the advance. It will give people a lot of faith in the incoming ruler."

"That was the last thing I wanted to discuss."

"Someone told you?"

He nodded. "The men did. It is my opinion that he doesn't have the background to make the best choices. There are the allies to think about, as well as our own armies. It's as much a job of managing people as it is about planning for the fight. How about we share the role?"

His mother's nostrils flared, very slightly. "Just make it easy for him. If you need to advise him, do so. That's the best you can aspire to now. You know that. Especially after The Trail of Tears."

"Very gracious of you," he said, swallowing back the response that came into his mind.

"No need for a rotten face," his mother said, treating him like some youth of eight decades. "You got what you wanted. I'll have Fennen write up the contract. Do you want tea?" She gestured to Tuel, who stood up.

"No, thank you. I've got things to do." He bowed as he left the room. She didn't need to know that the 'things' involved a visit to the destinarium.

⁂

HE ARRIVED DURING THE float again. Gwyneth was just coming through the door and she held it open for him. "You saved me a trip. Fennen sent me to give you this." She passed him a scroll. "It's the contract."

"Right," he growled, crumpling it slightly. Burning it would do nothing. The original had been written into faerie law and this was simply a copy.

"And ah, the court date is on the morrow. Don't look at me like that. Only the messenger," she said, holding up her hands.

He took off, unable to stand the heavy ground for a moment longer. He felt immediately lighter in the air, darting upwards through air currents. Tomorrow. Was there any reason for it to be so soon? He had no doubt that this urgency was designed to add stress, like thrusting them into a cauldron of boiling water.

Two could play at those mind games, he thought. But the next task would be a little more difficult.

Sneaking into his parents' chamber made him feel like a child. He threw a stone along the corridor towards the shutters. When the doorman went to investigate, he slipped in the door, shutting it quietly behind him. There was the remains of a magical fire in the hearth. It was disconcerting seeing the chamber empty, since there were usually at least two or three handmaidens in there, as well as the queen and his father. He half-expected Tuel to emerge from one of the rooms off the main chamber.

He entered the treasury, ignoring the small golden chests that were locked and headed for a dark wooden chest at the back. It was long and low and covered in a thin layer of dust that puffed up as he opened the lid. He searched through and pulled out a large bundle of fabric from near the bottom, wrapped it up into as tight a ball as he could, tucking it into his cloak, and left the room.

Voices in the corridor made him cast around desperately. There was nowhere to hide. The window. He rushed there, fiddled with the latch and pushed open the shutters, before launching himself into the air.

Far below, he spread his wings and breathed a sigh. Curse his mother for bringing up The Trail of Tears, a campaign where he had made a critical error in assessing the situation. It had cost them four good archers.

Aeban knew that he had been given the guard position to keep him happy about his brother being the heir to the crown. It was more than most younger siblings got. But he'd worked as hard as he could to become captain and he thought he did a bloody good job. Except for one large mistake.

It was convenient that now that he'd proven he could toe the line, he was no longer needed. Except as an advisor to his *frostbitten* brother.

Chapter 8

Cara

"Tell me of your made-up books. What sort of stories do you read in your world?" Aeban was in his accustomed position, sitting at the cool end of the chaise, while she was in the sunny spot. Cara turned to him, surprised that it was him asking the question this time.

"All sorts," she said. "I particularly like dystopian fiction, where the characters try to survive together in a world that's desperately against them. Ah, brutal worlds of corruption and..." She trailed off. "I also like fantasy books where the smallest, most insignificant character can make a huge difference."

He looked out the window. "No one person can change the world."

"No, I suppose not." Suddenly, her fantasy books seemed trite, when she thought of the world he lived in. "But I've always thought that the first step is to imagine something better. I know it's hard to see from within."

He stared hard at her. "Amusing that you make meaning from something that was made up completely. A lie."

"Yes," she said. "I suppose it might seem that way. But humans make meaning from literally everything. If someone who usually greets them doesn't do so one day, humans might think they were angry with them. Or they might think that person is having a really bad day."

"You could always just ask them." Aeban pointed at a picture. "This one is an image of our army before the Battle of Dreia's Bridge. Of course, it was called Gilded Bridge, back then."

"'History is written by the victors,'" Cara quoted. "That's what one of our leaders once said." She stooped to look closer at the picture.

"That's true. This man here is a hoot," he said, indicating one of the soldiers, who looked to be halfway shifted into a wolf, claws extending from his hands and his forearms covered in fur. "He'd just told us a joke about when—" He stopped as he saw her face.

The image was painted in dark colours. Menacing clouds took up the whole side of the page, obscuring the background. Dark horses carried fearsome riders, their faces twisted into war cries. A chariot carried a terrible warrior. Some wore no shirts and their hair streamed behind them. Wolves and hounds ran alongside. Huge birds flew above and behind. People fell away in fear of the oncoming army.

"You run with the *Wild Hunt*?" she exclaimed.

"Excuse me?"

"You know, the foaming black horses? Odin, Thor? That's your army?"

He shook his head, looking genuinely bewildered, and gave a light shrug. "I'm not aware of what you're talking about."

Cara sighed. It was a picture of the Wild Hunt, she was sure of it. Maybe her world just had some of the details wrong.

"Who is this?" she asked, pointing at Odin in his chariot.

"That," he said, proudly, "is Ombris. God of darkness and revenge. We had him with us that day, and his blessing helped us overcome when a darkening storm was upon us. It was one brigade up against three. I remember it well, although it happened some eighty years ago. The gods have been mostly silent since."

"If you don't mind me asking, how old are you?"

"We don't count the same way as you, instead counting moons and decades. I'm around twenty decades."

"Two hundred years."

He nodded. "Each decade has a different creature that governs its fate. At the moment, we're in the time of the dragonelle."

"So you and Alawynn were born in what decade?"

"In the time of the serpent. When I said, the other day, that I'm the younger of the twins, I spoke truly, of course. It was but an anomaly of translation. We call ourselves the younger when we lose our coming-of-age duel. The older sibling really translates to the one who inherits everything from their parents."

Cara's mouth fell open. "You lost a duel and now you... get nothing?"

"It's the way of things."

"Do you mind if I ask what happened?"

He shrugged. "It's not important. I lost."

Cara took a deep breath. "Don't get offended. But do you ever question the way you do things here in the realm? Like, really step back and look at it?"

"Of course," he growled.

ONE MORNING, WHEN AEBAN appeared outside her room, he had fabric draped over his arm.

"Have you brought fresh clothes?" Her heart leapt at the thought. Her own shirt was getting stiff with sweat and she didn't even want to think about all the hidden dirt in her jeans since she'd been kneeling and digging in the dust each day. How must her hair look? It was still in its braid but the ends straggled around her face.

But he didn't smile. "This is formal wear. For the court."

"Oh. Wait, I'm going to court again? Today?"

"I told you that we may show mercy. May I help you dress?" He stepped forward and held the dress up. It was a dark purple, intricately embroidered to shine in shades of blue and lavender. It seemed to flutter and shimmer like the wings of the faerie people.

"Why didn't you tell me?" She put her hands on her hips, but he didn't appear to have any ulterior motive. His face was open and empathetic. She supposed she would need help with the swathes of such delicate fabric and the fastenings. She had to face the court again with no mental preparation. Her pulse sped up.

"Trust that I would have if I knew in advance. It all happened rather quickly."

"Is it even going to fit?"

She took off her cardigan, shirt and jeans that she had put on so many mornings ago for the planting. How many days ago?

"It will."

He bent down and arranged the dress for her to step into. She put a foot in, feeling the cool, silky fabric. A hand stroked lightly up her leg as he pulled the dress up.

"Charming," he said. "I've taught you everything I could in the short time we had." He was speaking fast with an urgency that she had never heard before. "You will need all of that and more."

"Well, I thank you for that," she said.

When she put her arms in the sleeves, he fastened the dress behind her back, his touch warm and light. He came around in front of her and tucked her hair behind her ear, his face hiding a storm of emotion.

She looked down. "Wow, this really displays my..."

"Don't," he said, gruffly, and moved to leave, but a hand lightly brushed down the side of her body and lingered at her waist. He walked out, pausing at the door with one hand on the branches. After a second, he looked back at her.

"I believe you are powerful," he said. "Don't let them convince you otherwise."

She was excited to be one step closer to seeing her sister. But a strange emptiness hit her when she realized she would be leaving Aeban behind. She tried to imagine him in her world, his graceful form bent over at a computer, perhaps. Making small talk about the latest shows to binge. Waiting in line at the supermarket. Buying a latté at the local coffee shop. No, it was impossible.

"I'll be escorting you to court at dusk."

THE HUGE TREE STRETCHED up as far as she could see, its branches silver as moonlight. Far taller than all the other trees, it seemed to shimmer, so that she couldn't quite say for sure where it started and finished.

"This is what all trees were like, very long ago," he said, when they landed on the ground. "This one is thousands of years old."

"It's beautiful." Her voice was low. She remembered the legend of Randolynn and how he had created the whole kingdom with the gifts from the gods.

"I have to wait outside," he said, with a quick press of her hand.

"Alright," she said, awkwardly.

Two other guards peered at them curiously. The huge wooden doors opened silently as they came close, to reveal three more fae in white uniforms.

"Magenbound," Aeban said, and they nodded.

An unfamiliar guard leaned towards her. "No magic allowed in the court," he said. "Witch."

"I know," she said, and stopped, suddenly thinking that might be considered rude. Didn't they know she didn't have any powers here? "I mean, it is known. But I do thank you for the reminder." She bobbed her head.

The guard nodded, and stood aside. Cara caught sight of herself in a mirror as she passed. She didn't look like a librarian at all right at this moment. She looked regal.

She was ushered toward a seat at the back. Only the Queen's advisors were talking in a quiet whisper. They turned to look as she came in. She focused on her steps, and heard the sound of her hem swishing along the floor.

"What is the meaning of this?" came the Queen's voice, tight as an overtuned string. All feelings of confidence fell away and Cara stood there, feeling as if she was taking up too much space. "Why are you wearing faerie-made clothes?"

The queen looked hard at her. All of the things she had been told ran through Cara's mind. Should she answer? She decided to remain silent, as much as it hurt. Then the long lashes swept down and the queen looked away, the picture of courtesy once again, face impassive. But there had been a moment of truth there.

"Sit, child. You've been here three moons," she said, without looking at her directly, voice seeming to come from everywhere at once. "Have you learnt anything? I hope so."

Cara nodded, and took her seat, feeling the absence of her guard sitting next to her this time. Three young faeries stood and played a minor melody with their flutes pointed towards the centre of the room.

The court was dappled in light like a forest glade. It was cool and hushed and smelt fresh. She felt the energy fill her up again, quickly, and couldn't help but sigh in happiness. It almost felt like she was drunk.

"It's the trees," a pale young man offered from down the row. He had a long nose and strange, light eyes. "They're happy." He winked at her.

"Welcome, fair ones," the same short man with the goat horns said to the room. "Let us first do business, then we will dine."

"Daneen Everglade." The young man next to her sidled past, brushing against her skirts, then trotted forward, bending himself over to bow. He wore a long coat of some silky material.

The adviser with the long fair beard spoke. "You were trapped in a mortal's house." There were a few gasps.

"Yes."

"Tell us what happened."

"On the first night I arrived, I was hungry. I found a house that had lights on. I asked for food, as there was nothing left out for me. My stomach was gnawing at itself like the rats that scrabble in the forest. I set off a terrible alarm bell that froze me in place. When the lady of the house came out, she was red in the face. She said there wasn't anything in the house and she had to go to a market. I tricked her. I'm not proud of it, but I told her that apple trees would grow wherever she touched. She was excited, thinking she could grow an orchard in her garden. But my charm worked inside and out. A massive tree grew in her kitchen and broke through the wall, which meant I was able to get in."

People in the court made shocked noises.

Daneen looked around himself. "She must have had a faerie protection charm on the door, because as soon as I stepped inside, I was stuck."

"You've been gone for how long?"

"Eighteen years. It was only ten months or so, in that world. But far too long a time to be watching their oracle, Dr. Phil." He shook his head.

Cara did her best to hold in the laugh that was bubbling up inside her. Do not laugh. Do not laugh.

The Queen considered. "A young pixie. All that's green and growing tells me you've been missed here. If I look at the law, I can't find anything to punish. It is completely within our bounds to use words in such a way that enables you to get what you need. And besides, you've been punished enough. You can go."

The man dropped to his knees, and Cara thought he turned even paler.

"Oh dear. How shameful to be trapped in the mortal realm," someone whispered. "Even though he's free, he'll be an outsider."

"But how did he survive?"

"Must have been the charm that trapped him."

The next name to be called was Anemone of Clearwater, a name that thrilled Cara to the bone. A tiny woman walked out to the middle of the floor and stood on the stone, shifting from leather boot to leather boot. Her silver hair reached almost to the ground but as she looked around her, Cara saw that her face was strong and her eyes a steel blue.

"Using magic to divert a river in the mortal realm," intoned the advisor.

"That's not—"

The short man held up a hand. "We have all the naiads under a watch," he whispered to the queen.

"It was in self defence," she said.

"Guilty," Prince Alawynn said.

"Yes," the queen said. "A naiad should never use her powers in the mortal realm. Mortals have ruined their waters. I've seen it myself. We cannot let them know that we can help them. We'd be overrun."

"I had to protect myself—"

"Enough!" the queen said.

Two guards floated Anemone out of the court, and Cara's gut twisted uncomfortably. Polite, she reminded herself. Be polite. It seemed that there were no other rules more important than that. Don't have any opinions.

Now everyone was silent.

"The mortal witch."

Cara paced to the middle of the room as she had seen others do. She bowed. Polite. Restrained. Up close, the queen was even more beautiful and terrible.

"We have had you in the court once before. We again remind you to speak truthfully at all times. You were here for your sister? No other reason?"

"I would say that you are right. That is the only reason." Cara wondered if that was the wrong thing to say.

"You made a wish on her behalf?"

"Yes. I did."

"You wanted her to have a longer life than mortals are normally entitled to?"

A few people laughed but then covered their mouths.

"Well," she said, thinking desperately. That wasn't quite it. *Don't argue*, she thought. "Yes. I apologise for it."

"Hm," the queen said. "You tried to learn our secrets from my son? Someone saw you spying," she said when she saw Cara's face.

"No," she said. "That wasn't—"

"There's so much you don't know," the queen said. She put out one hand. "You haven't learnt anything about our ways. Take her back to the cells."

Cara's heart sank, and her legs almost gave way from under her. Two of the guard grabbed her arms and walked her towards the doors. She had a fleeting thought to try to escape as the doors closed behind her.

What was this? She felt a familiar strength in her core that told her she was one of many. She had bloodlines of magic inside her. She felt her power building in her hands and reached back towards the queen. She wanted to push her back, frighten her. Heat warmed her veins and sparks built as she drew magic. In a woodland realm, fire would be the one thing to strike fear in their hearts.

Several things happened at once. She felt as if her feet had fallen out from under her and a sick dizzy feeling came to her throat. One of the guards crumpled. The other one gripped her strongly by the wrist and with his other hand, he pulled the mirror off the wall.

Chapter 9

Aeban

“Take flight,” Menele, the court guard, said, gesturing with his spear. “Get out of here, already.”

Aeban only grunted. Walking felt as if he was dragging his feet through mud at the best of times. He longed to take off. He’d been pacing back and forth for what must be an hour.

Finally, he went to the door. A sharp spear tip pricked the soft flesh at the side of his throat.

“It’s me.” he said. “You know me.”

“The instructions for today were to make certain you did not enter. Specifically you. Do you want to join with the tree like one of your prisoners?”

“Alright. Alright.” He put up his hands.

Menele indicated the window, where Charming was sitting inside in the gallery.

“Apparently this one was digging her way out. Like some sort of mole. What was she going to do after that, though? Fall to the ground? Mortals, huh.”

That was about right. He had noticed that she always remained calm, got all the information and made a plan. He admired that about her.

It was always difficult to be around Charming but it had become more and more so in the last few days. That morning, he’d gone to her cell with every intention of spending all day teaching her how to be a good subject in the court. When he passed her the dress, he brushed her hand and it hit him like the morning sun. He did the dress up for her and caught her scent, of herbs and dirt and sweat and something uniquely her that was intoxicating, pulling.

He'd had the dress tailored so that it would expand to fit her curves. It showed her shoulders, her chest. He tried to keep himself from touching her, covering her body with his.

Everything inside him wanted to protect her, to put one arm around her small frame and take flight from the prison courtyard, leaving the tree and the whole rotten realm behind. But he swallowed hard and bid her goodbye. He had to get out of there so that he could breathe again.

Landing on the ground, his footfalls had been heavy. He hadn't taught her enough. The court appointment was too soon. She'd be eaten alive by them all.

Then he realized that he hadn't given Charming back her powers. That was another mistake, burn it.

He peered through the window into the court. Satisfaction warmed his blood as he noted how pale the queen was. He had known that his mother would be shaken by seeing Charming wearing that dress. It was made for the queen's sister on her coronation, which had never come to pass, of course.

He was one of the only ones who knew the real story of the Rose and the Rosehip. One of them was the presumed heir to the throne, an accomplished swordswoman, strategist and master of divination. She had spent years learning diplomacy in readiness for her role. And the other one was her sister, his mother, the one who gave her sister's bones to the tree and played fast and loose with the fates.

The magic of the Chalice, that was designed to be used to write wish contracts, to write prophecies and to make sure the fates were honoured to keep their deities happy, was instead used to make the realm look good and keep their allies happy. They spent their hours in the library designing plants not for practicality and beauty, but for weapons and defence.

He thought of the prophecy that his aunt spoke to him, on a dark evening, in the crypt:

'When a mortal appears as faerie, in the time of the dragonelle,

The throne will fall to a wish'

Later, he'd found out that his mother was listening that night, too. He'd used that to advantage, today, to try and keep the queen guessing, perhaps to make her feel a little off kilter. Judging by the look on the queen's face when she saw the dress Charming was wearing, it had worked.

But it was not enough. He rubbed the stubble on his jaw. Could he trust Charming not to use her magic in the court?

From his spot on the little hillock, he had a good view of the queen, his brother and the ambassadors sitting up the front. His father was sitting with his back to him. Unfortunately, the guards also had a good view of him. Menele kept glancing his way and was now murmuring to the other guard.

He risked another look. Whatever Charming had said made the queen's face grow taut and Alawynn sneered. Curse it. He knew that it was not going to go well and quickly stopped the diplomatic block he had on the witch's powers. She could not be locked away again. It wasn't right.

How long would it take her to realize? Her shoulders went back, confidently, and she lifted her arms. He saw tiny sparks appear.

Lumbris, she'd burn the whole cursed realm! Yes, he wanted to make a statement. But not like this. In a second, he made a decision. He stepped behind a tree and loosed an arrow towards the wall, so it would whistle past the guard. As the guard moved forward to see where it came from, he slipped through the door.

The guards there would be tougher. They had their backs to him, watching the prisoner. He pressed his back to the wall, clinging to the shadows. There was nothing for it. In for a silver, in for a whole dragon's hoard.

He pulled from his magic to create a portal in the mirror, breaking at least three rules in doing so. He pressed his foot into the back of the knee of the one on the right, who crumpled. Another two rules. The other one grabbed him, so he put his hand over the man's mouth and kicked his foot out from under him. The man fell, hitting his head. He grabbed the human witch and stepped into the portal.

Chapter 10

Cara

The landing was bumpy. Cara took Aeban's hand, gratefully and stood up. She looked around herself to see that the court had disappeared. They were in a small kitchen garden, with the scent of soil and green plants around them and the purple grey light of evening in the realm streaking the sky.

"What happened?" she asked, stupidly.

"You did a fine job," he said, packing things into a bag. "But she is neither fair nor kind. I saw that you were going to attack." He was walking quickly and she had to trot to keep up.

"Did you kill that guard?"

"No, but I had to make sure he couldn't follow us."

"But what will happen to you now? What were you thinking?"

"I wasn't really thinking," he said. "I've spent my whole life thinking. Working within our realm's rules to make change. Writing the histories of a family I don't agree with. Making their stories sound magical and heroic. Guarding and watching while they treat people with cruelty. Listening to those most impacted by their choices. Their whims." Aeban paced up and down, fists clenched, as he spoke. Then he turned and his wings folded slowly out. He made a terrible silhouette against the purplish clouds. "It would have been instant death for you if you attacked them. Or worse."

He set off at a fast pace around the edge of the building.

"Where are we going?" she said, when she caught up.

"We are going to ask for help from the naiads. Our allies will surely recognize the younger son of Queen Talynn. Even if I am no longer the captain."

"But we can't."

"Come on," he said.

"No, wait! I heard in the court that the queen has them under watch."

He frowned. "That is unfortunate. Then I'm going to send you back."

"I have to find my sister! And what will you do? You attacked a court guard."

He stopped, and she gratefully caught her breath. "She's here. Your sister is here."

"She is? How do you know?"

He sat on the low stone wall surrounding the gardens. His face was turned away, but she could see that his jaw was moving.

"I picked her up from your realm and brought her here. I made that portal that you came through. It was my duty."

"But I thought... I thought I was being held because I made a sacrifice? I thought you had granted my wish for her to live a long, healthy life. But I sacrificed ever seeing her again," she finished in a low voice.

"The queen drips mead from her lips that is sweet and intoxicating. That is sadly not what has happened. Your sister's wish was granted. I picked her up and delivered her to live with my brother here in the court. She will bear children for him. She made the sacrifice in order to have children. In return, she lives a life like anyone else."

Serena was to be married to the prince? No way, Cara thought. Not if she could help it. "You brought her here?" she asked, the bottom of her stomach dropping away as the realization of what he had said got through to her brain finally. "But she's really ill. Is she healed? Is she alright?"

Aeban gazed at her for a long moment, obviously assessing just how stubborn she could be. He let out a sigh.

"I'll take you to her."

Cara didn't speak as he made a portal, then reached for her hand and stepped through. Just as she thought that she must be getting used to this way of travelling, the vertigo hit her like she was spinning on the spot.

"Are you alright?"

She nodded. They raced along the corridor and Aeban stopped, listening.

"Alawynn will imprison us if he finds us," he hissed. "Follow me into this cache. You'll have mere minutes to talk to her and make sure she's alright and then we have to get far away from here."

Cara stepped into the wall through a shining door. Aeban's fresh citrus and sandalwood scent overpowered her in the small space. He shifted slightly, then seemingly turned to stone. She felt a warm hand against the small of her back. Cara didn't dare to breathe. Through a gauzy wall, she could see Serena.

Her sister was lying on the huge four poster bed, her pale arm dangling off the edge as white as the sheet. Prince Alawynn was talking to someone else.

After what felt like an age, he said goodbye to Serena and walked out the door.

When the prince left the room, Aeban opened the wall. Cara ran to the bed.

"Cara?" she asked, sleepily, then rubbed her eyes. "You're here?"

She sat up, pulling the covers up when she saw Aeban. Cara was happy to see that her sister's face was filled with colour and she was looking plump. "Are you alright? What have they done to you?"

"I'm fine. Don't worry."

She embraced her sister in a hug, then pulled back. She ran her eyes over the huge bed, the nightdress her sister was wearing, her rumpled hair.

"What? I'm an adult. I feel better than I've felt for a long time."

"Why was he talking to you?"

"He wants to marry me, but he's not going to force it. I certainly don't want to marry him. We're friends, though."

Cara raised her eyebrows. "Friends? And you're going to have children with him?"

Serena looked across at Aeban, who was standing by the window, peering through the gap in the shutters. "Who's this?"

"One of the guards. Don't change the subject. I'm just worried about you."

"I'm happy to see you."

Light footsteps came from outside the door, and Aeban motioned to hurry up.

"That's all very nice, but we've got to go. Now," she hissed, pulling on her sister's arm.

Serena lay her head back on the pillow. "I'm not going anywhere. I'm happy. How many people can truly say that? I feel the best I've felt in my entire life. My skin feels young again. I've got energy."

Cara searched her sister's face.

"It's a charm, it must be. Did you give them your name?"

"Well, I did. But I want this."

The door handle began to turn, and Cara stared at her sister. She had to believe her. Had to let her go.

"We must leave now." Aeban held out his hand and when she grabbed it, he stepped into the mirror. She followed, prepared for the unsteadiness this time.

They landed in a long branch house with cabins on each side.

She sat down against the wooden wall to wait for it to pass. Aeban offered her his hand to help her get up.

"There are worlds within worlds in this realm," she said. "Just like a library."

"This is the barracks of the Guard. Now just one thing." His eyes were dark. He grabbed her hands and brought his face close to hers, then kissed her roughly, quickly. He pulled away. "I will miss you, Charming. We must move quickly, as they will be able to sense the portal. They won't let you escape."

Outside, Cara found herself in the Auld Forest again. She wondered for a second whether he meant it when he said he would miss her. Then she realized that he couldn't lie, and felt a little thrill. It was immediately followed by a small, empty feeling as she realized she was going back to a world without Serena or Aeban. How strange would it feel to go back to the mundane and the busy?

He started running and she ran too, but he floated her along as the sound of wings came from behind and above. She was once again lifted off her feet, a strong arm around her.

Aeban stopped at a stand of trees with a creek running through and conjured a portal.

"Hurry," he said.

"But... " He grabbed the top of her arms and pushed her through, and she was falling.

She bumped onto the ground. Her hand slipped on something smooth and she lifted it up to see a silver crisp packet, and she felt a little nauseous. Rubbish. She looked around at the sparse pines. The plantation that was not a real forest. The planting that was needed because people had burnt up the hillside. Her eyes burned.

She stood up.

"Charming? Would you please come over here and help me up?" Aeban's voice cut through her thoughts.

She turned back to the clearing and was at his side in an instant.

"Why?" she gasped.

He turned his face to hers and she saw a huge wound that ran down his side and disappeared behind his back.

"My brother did it. He called me a traitor."

"But... can't you heal yourself?"

He shook his head.

"Okay. This is alright," she said. "This is fine. This is... I'll brew up some potions for you at home. I need arnica, St John's Wort, and comfrey—"

He smiled. "I knew you'd be able to help me."

"First, though, painkillers. But how will you get back?"

He shook his head. "I knew the minute that your wishes came through that night that I was involved. You, me, and your sister were all linked in some way. I denied it, even though I knew that I wanted you as soon as I saw that feisty woman with her hands on her hips, at Ynore's inn. I wanted you even more when I saw you in the court talking to my mother as if she was a mortal."

She smiled. "What did I sacrifice? I still don't understand."

"You sacrificed that person who has been most dear to you. Your sister. So that she could have her wish."

Cara nodded slowly. "I am going to miss her so much."

"I've never met a mortal who is as honest as you. And brave, interesting, and smart—"

"Alright, that's enough," she said, leaning down and stopping him with a kiss. It was a thorough one this time, and her hair dropped down on either side of their faces so that it made a little world all their own.

He squeaked and she jerked back.

"Oh, I forgot for a moment. I need to get you some codeine. First, I'll bring the car up. Can you walk?"

He reached out a hand and she pulled him up. Then he leaned on her to hobble through the plantation. "It's just a little further. But, I mean, how is this going to work?" Her mind was spinning and her mouth seemed to be working on its own too. There was a huge faerie man here in Ledstow, England.

He was looking far into the distance. "I need to spend a little time looking outwards, instead of magenwards. But what is the codeine?

And the car?"

She laughed. "Oh, that's just the start of it. Wait until you try a mocha latté with whipped cream."

Chapter 11

Cara

He looked too large in the dining room of her house, shoulders hunched as he stared out of the window into the small back yard. Brooding.

Cara had somehow got them home, grabbing the spare key from under the fence paling at the side of the house and unlocking the door. She took her time in the kitchen, bringing him water, pain medication and a handful of cashew nuts from the jar, since that was the closest to the food they had eaten together. It was also one of the only things she could trust in the pantry. The flat smelt a little bit musty from the—Was it days? Weeks?—since she'd been gone. The very air felt dryer, heavier. If she was feeling this way, she couldn't imagine how he felt.

She glanced over. His face was focused one hundred percent on the outside, staring into the tiny garden.

"How are the injuries?" she asked.

He shrugged. "Just a scratch." He went back to looking out the window, leg jiggling slightly.

"I mean to ask," she said. "What's next? What are you going to do?"

"What shall I do, now? Once I'm a little better, I'll be able to draw on my magic to open a portal. That way, they won't know where I'll arrive."

She sighed in relief. "Oh, you can do that?"

"Of course. Although it's not strictly allowed," he said, with a grin.

"What a surprise. There's a rule for that."

He went over to the window. "Look at this place. I've only ever visited on missions. Never had enough time to look around. It's intriguing."

What am I going to do with you? She thought. *I don't mind you staying for a few days but we kissed once and now you're moving in?* That kitchen hadn't seen a man since who knew when.

Cara had long ago decided that dating for her would involve two consensual adults who would go out for dinner, be truthful with each other about their expectations and wham bam, no strings attached. She'd be gone before breakfast, eager to get back to Serena to make sure she was alright.

"I might need to buy some food," Cara said. "There's nothing much here. I haven't got my phone, though," she mused. Would the market here in town be open? It could be a Sunday today. It could be any day, really. It was a very strange feeling, a sort of jet lag.

She opened her laptop to check the date and time. "The 6th of November? So we made our wish on Halloween. Then the next morning, I noticed Serena was gone. Five days?"

He grunted.

Five days. But it felt like when you finished a book that was so epic, so life-changing that you couldn't read anything else. You'd made new friends, gone on a journey with the characters, explored new worlds, mourning colleagues along the way. You had seen people become the best versions of themselves. You'd gained new understanding. And now you yourself were fundamentally changed because of that story. You were someone new.

It was surely weeks that she had been imprisoned in that gorgeous, vibrant place of floating blossoms and golden dust. She must have spent weeks looking for her sister.

Her sister. The thick, dark knowledge of loss came over her and she grabbed the edge of the bench. There was Serena's sketchpad where she doodled designs for her graphic design business.

No, she couldn't dwell on that. She had a giant whatever-he-was to look after. A guard of the royal winged army. A prince, she realized, with a start. Well, princes needed to eat, too. Finding food would be something to keep her occupied.

She took a shower in the upstairs bathroom, taking her time over conditioning her hair and watching the dirt wash down the drain, then towel-drying it before going downstairs. Had anyone ever appreciated hot water this much?

"I'm going to pop out and get some food for us," she said, in a bright voice that didn't sound like hers, and headed for the door. "What do you like to eat?"

Aeban looked up. "I'll accompany you," he said.

"No, there's no need. Really." His frown suggested that he didn't believe her, and she realized that this world was very different for him. She spread her hands. "There's nothing dangerous here in Ledstow. I'll just pop around the corner. I've been doing it every few days for most of my life. The only thing likely to get my heart going is the grocery prices. Really, it's fine. Your poultice needs time to work its magic, anyway."

"Your bravery is limitless, Charming. But I can't actually stop you, even if I wanted to."

She smiled at him and grabbed her purse off the hook then closed the door behind her. It would pay to get another key cut, she supposed. She grabbed the spare key and took it with her.

Ledstow was bringing its best, as the row of flats opposite hers was covered in vines with leaves ranging from green to a burnt orange to crimson. The school had just rung its bell and the children spilled out onto their field like round lollies rolling out from a bag.

She would get used to it again, she was sure. She saw a familiar face coming out of the supermarket as she went in. It was Lottie.

"Oh, Cara!" she said. "I've been calling your phone."

"I've lost it. I really should get another one."

"Are you alright? I've got to get back to the shop pretty quickly," she said, likely referring to her cafe. She lifted the bag up to show her that it was full of milk of different types. "But you could pop in for a pot of tea?"

"Maybe later. I need to get some food first. Then I've got a few other jobs to do." Like get my head back into this world, she thought.

"Will you be coming to the coven meeting?"

"When is it?"

"Oh. You don't know? It's on tomorrow night. There was an email. I thought I chatted about it with you a few days ago."

Cara tried to imagine the conversation that would ensue if she said that, for her, weeks had passed since she had seen Lottie, but settled for a simple response. "I'll try to make it."

"Hey, take care, love. You sleeping alright? Do you need an enchanted latte or something?"

"I'm fine. Thanks."

She waved goodbye, then went into the shop and browsed the produce section. What could be equal to the faerie realm grapes and oranges? They tasted so tender and sweet, juice bursting from every bite. She bought a loaf of freshly baked baguette, a bag of grapes, some apples, and a wedge of cheddar cheese, as well as a few other items to cook for dinner. Well, she could only do what she could do. She stopped into the locksmith's to get her key cut, then went to buy herself a relatively cheap phone.

When she got back to the house, she found Aeban looking at the Monopoly game that was in the shelf. He had opened the lid and was holding one of the silver gamepieces. He put it back when she opened the door.

She lifted the shopping bag onto the bench and started getting things out. "Now, we've got some fruit here, some bread and cheese..."

She put a few things on a plate for him and placed it on the table.

"Do you need to pay silver for food? Do you not grow any?"

She nodded. "Most people just buy food at the shops here. I do wish I had a little garden, though." Between her working hours and her witchy obligations to the coven, she'd somehow never found the time to start one.

"Only the poorest peasants wouldn't grow their own garden in our realm," he said. "It's certainly different here. But I want to learn more about this place."

"Well, I'm sorry that this is like a peasant's house to you," she said, laughing. That attitude. "It was just my sister and me... and it was fine for us..."

She fell into a chair, groceries left half-unpacked, forgotten, on the bench. Serena.

Now, there was time to think about it. That was always when it hit you, when you least expected it. When you were unpacking the groceries, and a subconscious rule whispered to put the fruit in a fruit bowl, because that was what Serena liked. She said it reminded her to eat fruit instead of snacking on other things. But what really ended up happening was that she would reach over the fruit bowl to get to the biscuits and then Cara ended up eating the over-sweet bananas and too-ripe oranges herself.

"Are you well, Charming?" He was sitting at the dining table, hunched over in the small chair, picking at grapes.

"You can't call me that," she said, perhaps avoiding the question.

"You seem even sadder than when you were up the tree." His voice was quiet. "Here, I'll put these in your larder."

Why was this so much harder than it was then? She had a plan then, she reflected.

She picked up the remote and turned on the television, slouching down in the puffy couch. A cooking show. Nice, light viewing.

Aeban leaned forward. "This is fascinating. Does your royal court use cooking battles to decide the succession?"

She giggled in surprise. There was so much to unpack in that sentence. "It does not," she settled for saying, "but this guy does think he's the king."

He came and sat on the couch next to her, not quite touching. As it grew darker, they watched the show together, his arm draped around her shoulders.

"Look at me," he said.

She did, and his eyes flicked to her mouth. She felt herself drawn to him, pulled. Her knees settled either side of his body. He looked surprised and held his hands up. She said nothing but, placing her palms face up and tilting her head back, she concentrated, teasing the magic apart to bring her energy.

Little fires sprang up around them in a circle of protection. His eyes widened.

He brought his hands around her back. She leaned in and kissed him.

It felt like she was getting closer to him by the day. Why did she feel like she understood him when she knew nothing about their way of life, their harsh rules?

It was a shame that it would make it harder to say goodbye.

SHE SHOWED HIM TO HER sister's room and changed the bed for him to sleep in. "You do sleep?"

"I do, but not for many hours, like you do."

"How many hours?"

"About a quarter of your sleep time. I'll be fine. There is a chair here. I shall sit and read your histories." He gestured to her sister's bookcase, which was messily arranged with books ranging from well-worn tomes of Goosebumps to true crime, stacks of magazines and celebrity memoirs. Her sister's taste in books was a little different from her own.

"Ah, don't put too much stock into what they say," she said. "They're probably more like a bard's tavern songs. Made to entertain."

In the event, he was in bed for eleven hours. She'd gotten up early and made breakfast, quietly, surprised that he wasn't awake. She'd never actually seen him sleeping before. Throughout the morning she checked on him more often, becoming afraid that she'd actually drugged him with the painkillers.

She crept into the room. His back was moving lightly up and down still, thank the goddess.

Cara glanced over his sleeping body. It looked like a Greek statue. Where did his wings disappear to? she wondered. How were they so powerful to lift him and her with no problem at all. What did his skin feel like just there, at the edge of the sheet. She bit her lip.

He jumped up as a loud noise drilled into the quiet. Wind whipped past her as he ran and crouched in the landing, light on the balls of his feet, looking for an enemy.

The speed that he'd moved took away her breath for an instant. She put her hands out.

"What? It's just a plane flying over."

His nostrils flared.

"It's alright." But whether she was reassuring him or herself, she didn't know. Everything inside her screamed a warning. He didn't seem to know she was there.

He slumped against the wall.

Chapter 12

Aeban

He kept his eyes shut, enjoying the sound of her voice.

"First aid," she said. "First aid. What did I learn from the first aid course? Scrape your fingers in their mouth so they don't choke on anything. Is that part of it? Airway. Breathing. Circulation. Breathing? Good." Her breath on his neck raised goosebumps. "Check the eyes for dilated pupils. Throw a bucket of water on them?"

He grabbed her wrist as she reached towards his eyes.

"Oh. Are you ok? Can you get to the bed?"

He flopped ungraciously onto the bed, pain searing his side as he did so.

"You need to stay there, please. What do you think happened?" She looked over his face, forehead creased in a frown.

He sighed, but leaned back against the headboard. "I fell. Like some green soldier new to the guard."

"You fainted? I'm sorry, but I think it could have been from the codeine I gave you."

He eyed her. "It's a poison?"

She swallowed. "It might work that way if it doesn't work with your body. I'm so sorry, I don't know anything about your people. I'm not really that good at the healing side of witchcraft, either. I've only learnt because of my sister."

He put his hand out. "You didn't know. It might also be because I'm here in your world."

"What do you mean?"

"We usually only visit for an afternoon, at the most. We get weaker the longer we stay away." He turned his face away, not wanting to tell her that she was also in more danger the longer he stayed away. Because of a choice he'd made.

She clucked her tongue. "Well, that's very convenient for a realm that needs soldiers, isn't it?"

"Sorry?"

"Don't worry. But you need to get back there, then."

IT WAS THE NEXT DAY when they ventured out for a walk through the town. He begged her to show him around.

She noticed that he put on his quiver underneath his clothes and held his bow.

"You do know that I'm a witch?" she asked. "I won't say it's entirely safe here in Ledstow, but you'd be hard-pressed to find many nicer towns. But if your wound starts hurting, we're coming straight back."

They walked along the river bank and she pointed out flowers and told him stories of their town.

"What is that?"

"It's a weights machine. For getting healthy."

He dipped down next to the river, on one knee, and trailed his fingers in the water, listening. He was about to lick his finger when she stopped him by grabbing onto his hand.

"I wouldn't," she said, grimacing. "There's all sorts in there. Disease."

"But how do you know the river otherwise?"

"I guess we don't. Why would you need to know the river? Oh, look at that," she said, pointing to a mess of what looked like leaves and rose petals floating towards them. "Do you see that?"

"What is it?" he asked, watching it float past.

"It's a word." Cara gasped a breath. "It's from my sister. It has to be."

"Why do you think it's from her?"

"It plainly spelt out Viola. When we were children, there was a detective show that we used to watch. She would always call herself Viola after one of the characters. I'm not just seeing signs of her everywhere because I miss her," she said, somewhat defensively.

"It's not that at all. I simply wondered why she would send a message of that name. Of course a river could be used as communication from our realm. Anything reflective can be. I thought you would have known that from all your reading," he teased. "It likely connects to a mirror in the castle. But she must be sending that same message out fairly regularly for us to come upon it."

"So she is trying to contact me. She needs me."

"I can see you're worried."

"Well, an hour here could be a day or even longer for her."

Aeban lapsed into silence, until a rustling alerted him. Burn it. He whipped her out of the way, just as something whistled past.

"Ouch," she said.

He loosed three, four, five arrows into the trees in the commons.

"Stop. What are you doing?"

"Stay there," he said. "There are members of the royal guard nearby."

Chapter 13

Aeban

He was already running before he finished speaking, ears pricked to hear the lightest sound. If only he had scouted out this area beforehand. He cursed his poor preparation. He didn't know the hiding places around this field.

Crouched low behind a metal box, he sent his senses out to search for danger. There, behind the shaggy bush, was a slight blurring which indicated a glamour was being used. It was definitely a pair of soldiers, but he couldn't be sure who it was.

They'd sent the arrows as a warning. Otherwise, he wouldn't be here now. Again, he cursed his lax attitude, allowing Charming to be out in the open like that.

He looked around. They were waiting for him to move first. He loosed an arrow to the left at the same time as rushing right. It gave him a second's grace to get behind the shed, which he decided was some sort of toilet, based on the smell.

There was no stopping now as he rushed from tree to tree, loosing arrows as he went. It worked to lure them out. He reached behind and realized this was his last. He nocked it and aimed for the fuzzy long shape that he assumed was an arm.

Aeban came running back to Cara and bent down to look. Her calf had a tiny trickle of blood. "I got one in the arm and knocked the other one out. It was Menele. It's the second time I've attacked him in as many days." He bent down to scoop her up.

"Stop. I can walk."

He spread his hands. "We always carry our fallen friends," he said. "I meant no offense. Now, that mark on your ankle is from our slim arrows. They are meant to stop our enemies still and prevent them from moving, while we await orders. Halt them. If they'd wanted an arrow to strike you, it would have."

"I can believe that. Did you know they were coming here?"

He shrugged. "I knew they wouldn't give up. We never leave a member of the guard behind. So they will be coming for me. No matter what. I should have told you about it. They'll only come through two at a time. That's how many a portal lets through and they take a lot of magic to create. We've got some time but they will be back."

"What are we going to do? We can't let them wreck the town! And we can't fight them. They know where I live!"

She was mortal. How many times would he have to watch her get sick or have accidents? And the reality hit him that one of them would be her last. "I have been thinking over what to do."

"You could have asked me what I thought," she said.

"I should have, I'm sorry." He looked side to side as he walked. "We're going to do what they least expect. We're going back."

Chapter 14

Cara

They arrived through the portal on a low hill, next to a well. The great tree was in front of them and the mountains rose up to her right. She still wasn't sure she was making the right decision coming back, but A Plan was always a hundred times better than No Plan.

"It's almost the float," Aeban said. "Dusk. I never know what time it will be when we arrive. You'll need some sleep, I suppose. But, first of all, I need you to be able to see what I see. Is that alright?"

Aeban lifted his hand and drew his fingers lightly across her eyelids.

Her mouth dropped open as she stared around. The great tree was gnarled and twisted, a creep of black rising up through the wood from the bottom.

Cara's eyes flicked to the city at the base of the tree, which looked rundown and shabby, as if a giant hand had given it a shake-up.

"What do you think of the great city of Epicotia now?" He watched her face. "The Queen is synonymous with magic, the most important force in the land. And the tree is the source of all magic. If the people saw this, there'd be absolute chaos."

"But... what? How did you do that?"

"What you saw originally is a sort of glamour that keeps the queendom looking strong and the city looking prosperous. Everything magenwards appears as you want to see it. I simply removed the veil."

"But you... your people can't lie," she said, slowly. Her mind was struggling to make sense of it. "How do you keep that hidden?" She was

95

disgusted at the difference between the world she'd seen and the world as it was.

"Most don't know. We've cultivated rules over many years for what we can discuss, the topics we bring up. Everyone in the city follows this etiquette, because there are consequences otherwise." He set off down the hill. "People are outcasts and they have to live further out. They wouldn't be able to live magenwards. They struggle a lot more as they get less access to magic. I've talked to a lot of prisoners over the years who tell me their stories of how they get there. What leads them to be so desperate as to make a wish."

"So it's not just humans who are left to rot in the prison?"

"No, it's not. Many, many of our people are taken in. Some are shown mercy. Those who know the truth are the scribes, some of our seers, professors, and the royal family."

"And what would happen if you wrote about it?"

"The scribes are kept under the strictest surveillance. We have a mycelium network that keeps the queen informed."

"Fungi?" It sounded like once you knew about the city, there was no going back. "But you've shown me now," Cara said.

"Yes," he said, simply.

She lapsed into thought. "And how do they cast the glamour?" she asked after a minute, trotting to catch up, as he picked his way deftly through some low shrubs, seeming to almost float along. If Cara was doing magic on this scale, she'd probably need a whole village of witches and a lake for a cauldron.

"Ah, now. You may have noticed that one of the queen's titles is Holder of the Magen? The Magen refers to a relic, a small gilded pot that's one of our greatest—"

"The Chalice," Cara put in. "See, I was listening."

He nodded. "The Chalice. The queen uses its magic to keep up this huge glamour all the time. It takes tons of magic. It also translates all languages in the realm so that we can all speak to each other;

ambassadors, allies, entertainers. There used to be travellers, too, back in the day. Hundreds of them. Oh, burn it!" This last growled exclamation seemed to be a curse, as they rounded the corner to the city gates.

The gates were sitting open but there was no way through. Jugglers threw balls high into the air as they rode along on what looked like buffaloes down the middle of the road. Dancers weaved in and out, their hair standing up in blue, green and silver tufts, seemingly unfazed by the beasts stamping their hooves nearby. People with antlers grew bright blossoms on their hands and blew them up into the air.

"What's going on?"

"The Rising."

"Oh," she answered, none the wiser. "Can we maybe fly in?"

"I want to avoid notice. The easiest way is going to be to try to blend in."

"To that? It looks pretty hazardous." Cara was sure she'd get trampled, or at the very least, get an antler to the face as the crowd swayed and pushed.

"It's a festival. The crowd will only be on this side of the gates. It will be fine."

She nodded. She could possibly manage to make it through the three metres of the crowd leading up to the gate, although she couldn't see how it would be any different on the other side.

He took her hand and led her into the throng of people. She could hear the distant beat of drums. Was this the part of the story where they got split up? She held tighter to his hand.

He threaded effortlessly between people, anticipating their every move, as if the crowd wasn't flesh and blood at all, but shadows. Cara apologised as she stood on the foot of one of the jugglers because she was looking up. The balls they threw so high were silk and left shimmering trails of silver behind them.

She came very close to being squashed between what looked like a buffalo and the cold stone of the gate wall was biting into her back. The beast stunk of mud. but Aeban came and pushed her backwards through a gap before the huge buttocks swung to the left where she had been standing a second before. The rider waved a banner that had a winged insect on it. It flashed for a moment then turned invisible.

As she emerged from the other side of the gate into the bright sunlight, she was amazed to see that the road was still busy but more orderly, although that might have something to do with the four fae guards standing still as statues as the crowd streamed by.

Aeban seemed to camouflage into the crowd and she concentrated on not falling over as she looked around in wonder. Vines hung across the street, with huge trumpet-shaped flowers, each one containing a tiny fairy that was playing music.

This! This was exquisite.

"In here." Aeban pulled her around a corner and into a doorway.

Cara looked around. It was a busy tavern and Aeban was jostling her through as quick as possible. Some fae were playing at a game of stones that were painted in red and black on a low table, accompanied by a lot of whooping sounds. The person, who she guessed was the bartender, judging by his dirty apron, was keeping an eye on the winner, holding a large flagon ready to put it down and take some of the winnings. The flagon seemed completely unnecessary at this point, as the winner had just snuggled his face into his neighbour's shoulder, out for the count.

Aeban rapped on the bar as they went past and slipped out a door in the back. It was only a moment until the huge bartender joined them.

"What do you want lad?" he boomed. "I've got punters out there and the only thing better for my business than a heartsore man is one who is feeling lucky."

"Alright, well you know how I've helped you out before..."

"That's never a good way to start a conversation." He winked at

Cara.

"We need a place, Diggins," he said, "just for the night. There are people everywhere. I wasn't prepared."

"There's a festival going on, if you hadn't noticed," he responded.

"I've been away. I'd advise you to cast your mind back to those many times when I've helped you with fighting patrons."

The bartender inclined his head. "Look, if you hadn't helped me by writing that testimonial after my ale was cursed, I wouldn't consider it. But you well know that saved my business. I'll get a message sent out to the guild. If you've got sufficient silver, most things can be done." He stomped over to the door.

"Cursed?" Cara asked.

"A punter thought that he was rigging the game of stones. So they cursed every cup of ale that passed across his bar. He managed to get the curse removed, but people still stayed away. I simply wrote a testimonial about what a great tavern it is and nailed it to the door."

"Oh, that was nice of you. All of that because they thought he'd rigged the game?"

One side of his mouth quirked up. "I never said he didn't."

Chapter 15

Cara

At the inn, they were greeted by a little old lady who looked, at first glance, as inconsequential as a leaf. They had walked to the edge of the city, Aeban finding the best path to avoid the guards. Revellers' voices reached them from the taverns. Some people sat outside on long trestle tables in the city squares, watching the blossom fall.

"What's The Rising all about?"

"It's a festival that's been happening each year during this decade. It's got bigger and bigger."

At the end of a long, narrow alleyway with buildings leaning towards them on both sides, they passed under a dark arch. Aeban knocked on the door of the inn. The woman opened the door and invited them in.

"Come in. I'm Maerie se Halda and my man is about here somewhere, too."

"We sent word through Diggins about a room?"

"Yes, of course," she murmured. The next moment Cara clapped her hands over her ears as the woman screamed.

"Donil! Donil!" She turned back to them, eyeing Aeban. Cara removed her hands, slowly. "We don't see your kind around here very often."

"Yes, I'm showing the lady around."

"Is that what they call it these days?" She said in a quiet voice, with one raised eyebrow. But she put her hands up in a gesture of innocence when Aeban glared at her.

"You have silver?"

Aeban nodded. They waited in silence, until the man called Donil arrived at the door and they followed him up the steps. Good, the room looked to be inside. At least they didn't have to sleep in the stable.

Cara went into the room first and collapsed on the bed. Aeban locked the door behind them. The room was large but simple, with one huge four-poster bed and one table. Light came from a small bluish fire.

"Okay, I have so many questions about all of this that I feel like I'm about to burst. But I really can't be bothered with the follow-up questions I'll have from all of your half-answers right now."

"It's no time for questions. You need food," he said. She was about to protest but her stomach drowned out her words.

He returned with a small but hearty dinner of stew, spiced with something that warmed the stomach and the heart, which they ate from the bowls, slurping every last drop.

Afterwards, she put her bowl away and lay back on the pillows. All of the walking and the adrenaline of the few days made her limbs heavy.

"I'm going to take the bed. You wake me up whenever you need to sleep." She yawned.

"I will not," Aeban said, but Cara was too tired to register. It would probably be ages before she could get to sleep, she thought.

Cara awoke to the sound of a rooster crowing. She couldn't move. Thoughts of curses flew idly around her mind, scattering when she realized that a warm, heavy arm was draped across her body and a large hand cupped around her left breast.

For someone who supposedly hardly slept, he sure slept a lot. She snorted to herself, but had to admit it was sort of nice waking up next to someone. It had been a long time. She didn't have any desire to get up. In fact, she was a little afraid to move as he might jump out of bed ready to attack, like he had back at her flat. But he seemed pretty relaxed at the moment. She could get used to this.

"Good morrow," he said, sleepily, blinking slowly. He moved his body against hers, and she squeaked.

"Oh, I am sorry," he said. He jumped up, shirtless and magnificent, dressed in only his loose pants. "I'll go and ask for some stew to break our fast."

"You might want to wait a minute," she said. It was good to know that things appeared to work the same in this realm.

He looked down and adjusted himself, with a quick grin at her.

When he returned with bread and cheese, Cara tore off a hunk and bit into it. It was like a cross between a rye bread and a wholemeal bread, fluffy and freshly baked with plenty of flavour. The cheese was a sharp, slightly orange, buttery wedge. It was all thoroughly delicious.

When they had finished, Aeban stood up, brushing crumbs from his clothes.

"I shall go and check where your sister is. Wait here. Don't move." He looked back to make sure that she was listening.

"Yes, fine."

"I won't be longer than an hour. Don't talk to anyone."

She threw him a withering look. There would be plenty to keep her occupied in the bright kitchen garden below the window.

She made her way downstairs through the deserted inn and to the door. What had caught her eye was sunflowers of all different colours planted along with parsley mint and some other herbs that she couldn't identify, a colourful mess of plants growing up two sticks in a pyramid.

But before she went outside, she stopped at a silver piece of art on the wall. It was the great tree and its reflection with the city of Epicotia at its base, all in relief. It looked to be engraved in some silver metal.

"Did you make this?" she asked Donil as she saw him pass, lugging a piece of furniture.

"Oh no, milady. We had to get an artist approved by the court." Approved by the court. Of course.

"Donil!" The shout came from the kitchen, and he hurried off.

Cara stayed to look at the engraving for another few minutes. It was not an exact likeness of the city, from what she could tell; perhaps the towers a touch taller, the fortifications a touch wider.

The sunshine warmed her soul when she stepped outside. She trailed her fingers gently over a huge purple and blue cabbage.

"That one's my favourite," Donil called.

She must have looked alarmed, because he approached her slowly.

"Is it ok if I talk to you? I love it when someone's interested in plants. Beyond the normal carrots and spuds. You plant it together with sage."

She nodded. "I must say I haven't got a garden at home. But I'd love to start one."

"Nothing better," he said. "Get out of it, Merv." This was said to a sheep that was leaning over a wooden gate, nibbling gently on one of the plants. But the man pulled out a bushel of grain and offered it to the sheep. "This is a weed. He can eat as much of that as he likes."

Cara couldn't help but think of Nate and tears pricked at her eyes.

"We were never blessed with children. The gods have been absent these decades, so I think a lot fewer of us were. Bit of a shame for our generation. The garden is full of my wee ones. Feed them and water them, just the same, and even sort out fights between siblings, when they're fighting over the sunshine. Although, these kids don't steal the family horse and take it on a joyride. This one's blueberry greenthistle. It makes a great tea for getting the mind moving. With a little lemon juice and a touch of cinnamon, it's perfect. Look at how hardy he is. We need to draw a little magic for the growing too, since we've got stony ground here."

"Do you? That's interesting."

"Of course, we have to balance it with the magic we draw for the stove. There's not a lot available but Maerie is pretty good at budgeting."

"Can't you just make a f—

"Shh," he said. "Those are banned. Don't you know?"

She shook her head.

Aeban came through the door and Cara's heart rose for an instant. But Serena wasn't with him. He glared at Donil, who stammered out an "Afternoon, your royalty," and backed away.

Aeban came up close to her, searching her face.

"Alawynn is with your sister at the moment. We will go and pick something up first and then we can seek her out."

Cara tried to pretend she was as confident as him. "Right. Sure." But her cold fingers told her she was like a fly headed straight for a spider's web.

Chapter 16

Cara

"Come in this way," he said, setting her down and opening a door in the side of a huge part of the trunk of the great tree. Up close, the trunk was as wide and forbidding as a city wall but the surface undulated like any other tree, so that there were outdoor rooms as large as fields in between. Huge toadstools grew up way above their heads, covering them with a dark brown fleshy canopy and an earthy smell. Cara wasn't sure if the door in front of them was there before or if he'd just created it. It was about two metres above the ground.

She slipped through into the gloom and the fresh and earthy scents of the forest grew deeper. "Is this the back door?"

"You might call it that." He shut the door softly.

Darkness surrounded her. "Why isn't it guarded?"

"Because of the festival."

She felt her way forward. The light was sort of bluish but she couldn't see the ground in front of her. And where was he?

"You can't see at all?" he asked, sounding amused.

Cara knew she must be leaning forward with her arms out and felt foolish.

"Can you see me?" she asked, grumpily. "That's hardly fair."

"*Eil su'a radinn, varad,*" he said, and she felt a warm hand wrap around hers. "It means, 'I've got you, brother.' It's what we say to each other in the guard." He continued as she shuffled along. "One of us always steps in to help if someone needs it. We wouldn't last long if we didn't know each other's weaknesses."

"I'm no brother. But I appreciate it." Cara followed along behind and her eyes gradually became used to the dark. It was a surprise when they came out into a wide corridor that was lit with clumps of what looked to be blue fire. As they got closer, she realized it was a phosphorescent fungi.

"It can mean sibling or teammate. Just stay as close behind me as you can," he said, and just as she was wondering why, the corridor turned abruptly and opened into a huge hall with sunlight filtering in through branches above. The floor seemed to be tightly compacted soil and paths wound up the edge of the hall and into the darkness beyond.

She hovered at the edge of the tunnel. There didn't seem to be too many people around, just a faerie hurrying down one of the other edges and a couple standing in the middle, heads together.

"Come on," he said, and disappeared. Well, not so much disappeared, she decided, but blended in with the background and glided along the wall. She stuck as close to him as she could, feeling like a book shelved in the wrong aisle. Slightly too large and the wrong shape. Someone would spot her, she thought. Or hear her. But no one did.

"I can't believe we got away with that," she said, once they finally reached the darkened corridor on the opposite edge and she could see his outline.

"They know we're here, although they're not exactly looking for us," he said. "But that doesn't mean we stroll right up to them."

Cara felt he was holding something back. Why would the queen not want to talk to them straight away? Or, at least, threaten them in that sweetly passive aggressive manner? Not even a summons from a minion? She laughed to herself.

"What's funny?"

"Nothing. Where are we going now?"

"I need some information about the plant that guards the chamber where your sister is. She has been moved from where she was before."

"Was she alright when you saw her?" she asked, quickly.

"Yes, she was," he answered, then they lapsed into silence. Cara ran her fingers over the rough stone wall as they spiraled downwards.

"You like stories so much," Aeban started. "I'll tell you one. It's the tale of The Chalice and the Stone.

"You told me that one, already."

"There's more. You know how the god Lumbris gave Randolynn three gifts? Well, the Stone sprouted and grew a great tree that had the strongest of timber. It grew larger than the rest of the forest. At the same time, a great city broke through the ground below. It was a perfect reflection of the tree. It contained a wonderful library, the heart of the city. In the library was a rotating depiction of the fates on the ceiling, made of gems and gold. It was the most detailed map of the destinies. This was to be the heart of all knowledge.

The Chalice was kept there. Lumbris told Randolynn that it was up to him to create all of the creatures, insects, birds and plants to make this the most beautiful land in the world. He could dip into the magic and create a world where no one was left behind, where peoples were welcomed to talk together and knowledge was shared. The Chalice was to be used to read the fates and make sure they were honoured to keep the gods happy.

Some people think the story of The Chalice and The Stone is about knowing where you come from and carrying that with you like a fortress or castle inside will give you strength. There are others who say it's all about keeping staunch and never giving up, of course. Some think it's a tale about how far you have to travel to realise where your home is."

The corridor they were in now was open along one side with a short guardrail made of carved wood, exquisitely detailed in designs of peacocks and winged creatures. Cara stepped to the edge to look out to see where they were as she was sure they were going downhill. She caught her breath.

They were in a huge... well, it was a well, she realised. Above them, the bluish sky was partially covered by the huge tree roots. A draft tickled the hairs on her arms. The pathway looked to spiral around the edge and the bottom held a silver whitish dome. Two waterfalls cascaded down on the opposite edge.

"We call this a *soursinn*, which can mean a well. Or, confusingly, a tower." He put his head on the side as if contemplating the language.

"It's ridiculously elegant." She turned back to drink it in. "And what's down there?"

"A great tree, reflected. One above to house the people. One below to house the stars," he said, as if reciting something. He pointed down. "Down there is the real library."

THE BOTTOM OF THE WELL branched off in three directions and Aeban didn't hesitate. He took a corridor and it opened into another huge room, which she thought must be under the dome that she could see from above. Columns stretched to the roof, painted with some sort of shimmering moving scene. At the foot of each column were altars with scrolls attached to them. People were writing with quills and dark purple letters appeared on them. Lanterns with bluish light hung from slender arms above their heads. No one had noticed them yet.

"Oh, this is not a library," she whispered. It was elegant and impressive, yes but it did not make you want to come in. Where were the comfy cushions and the quiet nooks? The welcoming smiles and the children reading?

"This is where all the scribes work. It's the official library and destinarium."

Feathers rustled and there was a flurry of pecks at the glass dome and birds flew in, chattering.

"What's that?" she asked, but he laid his finger along his lips.

"That was a wish," he said, simply.

Cara watched everything. She watched the concentration on one of the scribes' faces. "What are they writing?"

"Everything. They write to satisfy the realm. They describe the tree and the court, the gatherings and the people, the food and drink. Old things and new." He bent down and pointed to a spot just inside the door. "Now stay here. Or I will hunt you down." At least, that was what she thought he said.

Cara sat down behind one of the columns, drawing her knees up, resenting his words, her cold bottom on the flagstones and her empty stomach.

"Aeban," a strong voice greeted him. "Brother."

"How are the words flowing?" Aeban asked, in what seemed to be some sort of greeting.

"The words are fine," he responded. "Fine, fine. We've missed your ideas round here. Been busy with the fight?"

She saw Aeban pause and his hand came up to his jaw. "No, I've been... travelling, man." He moved his head closer to his friend and Cara strained to hear. "I'm looking for a specific scroll," he said. "A scroll about this decade's most practical botanical weapons."

The man, who was a dark-skinned fae with dread-locked hair, looked hard at him. "Are you sure?"

"I am allowed to, you know," Aeban said. "I'm the captain of the guard."

"You know it's not generally allowed," he said. "I'll have to inscribe your name."

"Really, Fennen?"

The man left the room and Aeban darted a glance over at her, so Cara stuck her tongue out at him.

Another woman came up to Aeban and chatted about the work.

"What are you working on?" he asked her.

"I'm just about to complete this one. Three scribes. Two moons' worth of work. Is there any point, though?" she sighed.

As she watched, the woman unrolled the scroll and placed it face down onto what looked like a bird bath. She seemed to gently press it down into the liquid, then stepped away.

A low sound emerged from the birdbath and a dark purple spark popped. Lavender flames emerged from it and burnt bright before disappearing.

The woman shrugged and sat down hard on one of the stone chairs. "See?"

"Yeah," Aeban said. "Don't look at me like that. I don't have any say in it, Gwyn."

Just then, the other man came back with a sack of golden fabric. He pulled out a large book and placed it on one of the altars. He started writing in it.

"Thank you, brother."

Aeban took the book and sat in one of the booths along the side of the room. An arching wooden cage came down from nowhere and slammed into the ground around the booth. Cara froze. Goddess.

Aeban was caught. His face seemed calm as he read the pages and he didn't seem too worried. She bit her lip.

After what seemed like an age, he signalled to the librarian and the cage lifted off. He walked straight back out of the library and into the corridor, without looking behind to see if she'd come. She scrambled up and followed him.

He was waiting for her beside a fountain. "Take a drink if you like."

She had a taste of the cool, fresh water to whet her parched mouth.

She stood up and faced him. "So are you going to tell me what that was all about? The scroll, the sparks, all of it. The cage?" She waved her hands, encompassing all of the happenings in the library. "None of that goes down in our libraries. The worst we have is when the public toilet gets blocked."

"Of course I'll tell you. The scribes do what they do best, writing poetic scrolls in there. They work in groups, inspiring each other. I sometimes work down there as well. But I don't have as much time for that since the latest offense has started. It's long hours for them, working right through the night, and thankless work. When we finish a piece, we cast it into the waters. It's either destroyed or put into the queendom libraries. Gwyneth's piece was destroyed then, as you saw."

"Right. And why would they not accept it? Who's making the decisions?" But she already knew, of course.

"The court. I once thought I could make change that way, but it has become apparent that I cannot."

"And what about the cage?"

"That's how we ensure people do not steal the scrolls. You're a librarian, aren't you?"

"We take their details and issue them a card," she said, lamely.

"And that's enough to ensure no one steals the stories? What if someone loses a book?"

"We eventually make them pay for the value of the book. And who was the guy with the... ?" She made a movement indicating short horns.

"Fennen is the Chamberlain of the Magen and Head Librarian. He fiddles with the numbers, although he doesn't like it if I say that. He allocates magic."

"Right."

He studied her. "One more question." he said. "That's all."

"All of that for a scroll?"

"Correction. Two scrolls."

HE LED HER DOWN A CORRIDOR with a sign that said, 'Wish Fufillment Science', and opened the door. They were in a sort of lecture theatre with rows of wooden pews.

She slid gratefully into one of the seats, while he pulled out the scrolls and pored over them. After a while, he put his chin on his hand and stared into space. He was silent for so long that the sound of his voice shocked her.

"This used to be a great university with many departments. The queen was a patron of the university but she withdrew her money, saying we needed to focus on outwards sciences, expanding the realm. That meant that she wanted us to focus on weapons and wartime tools. That was a very long time ago. Now there is a much-reduced faculty and only a few approved departments."

"Okay, that sounds like it was amazing. You should petition the queen to grow it again."

"I brought you in here to talk to you. I'm particularly aware that we are going to get your sister and get you out of here," he began, then stopped, leaving the rest unspoken.

"We'll have to say goodbye again," she said. "If we weren't leaving for different worlds after we rescue Serena, what would you do?"

He rushed to her, leaving her breathless and took her hand. "Can't you tell yet? What I want to do is lay you down in the middle of the Auld Forest. I'd feed you sweet grapes and lay my lips on every inch of your body. I'd worship it under the float, petals falling around us in timeless ecstasy."

Something tightened inside her. She swallowed.

"Oh."

"I will claim you as my own, *miran*."

He talked like they were together, like they had a future.

"What do you think is going to happen?" She asked with a half laugh. "Besides the fact that we hardly know each other, you belong to the sky and me to the earth. You belong here in a fairy tale world."

"That's a very interesting question," he said in response. "You know I have to answer you truly. Do you want to hear what I've got to say?"

Cara's breath caught at his expression. His eyes were burning into her as if he saw the depths of her soul. She was suddenly afraid but that made no sense.

"I will protect you with my bow and knife and my body if needed, from this day until we are done. I'll wait for you here until you return to me."

"I don't need protecting," she said, cursing herself. If this was in a movie, she'd be swooning right now. "What does *miran* mean?"

A slight smile softened his expression. "Then I will love you for each and every moment that we breathe and we will fight side by side for your happiness and peace. Miran means my own."

Cara looked down at her hands. She simply had no concept of what he was talking about. When she was younger, she'd had a misguided version of love in her mind. She'd thought that love could be found on her street corner.

She got into a relationship with her oldest friend, Stu, the baker's apprentice. But she soon found out that he didn't want any part of a life filled with witchcraft and caregiving. He didn't want her to care for her sister, didn't want to share. Her life, her very identity was something strange that didn't fit into his world.

She had decided that from then on, she was in control. Nobody would break her trust. Nobody would make her feel that way again. And it worked pretty well. She'd had one night stands. Goddess, it had even happened with the barista from the library cafe, once or twice. But to envision a life together with another person was something she could hardly wrap her head around.

Her life, living with Serena, had to be meticulously planned. There were systems in place, contingencies. She accompanied her sister to medical appointments, looked after her when she was worsening. They were a way to take some control over something so large.

Aeban unfurled a scroll and spread it over the table.

"Come here."

"What's this?"

He drew his hand over it and sparkly symbols rose into the air above the scroll. Tiny spheres with letters in between turned and bobbed gently. Cara gasped. With a pinch and drag motion of his fingers, Aeban zoomed into a section of the model and even more twinkling spheres jumped out of the gaps.

"This is what we call a fate map. It's basically a map of the celestial bodies. Reading these is one of the oldest sciences we have, like a language. We read it to find out people's destinies and sometimes, when we need to, we make sure they happen." He cupped his hand under a small section of the floating stars. "This group is the section that governs the faerie realm and there's a cluster of stars for each of our families. This one here is mine." It was a small, brightly burning pinkish star, surrounded by others that were less bright, one that was bluish, one that was golden.

"That is truly amazing."

"The fate map pops up like that for our blind people. They can run their hands over it and it will say the names of the clusters."

She nodded.

"You might like this part. This is the map for a couple of moons ago. It had been unchanged for decades."

He put another scroll on the table and the stars' positions changed.

"This is mine over here." He scooped one out of the air from in front of her and she recognised the pinkish star. "It all changed the night you arrived in the realm."

"What does that mean?" Cara asked.

"I've been waiting for the last piece of the puzzle. I finally figured out that this collection signifies the god Lumbris." He made another star bigger. When it was the size of a tennis ball, she could see that it was a blob of light, filled with tiny golden, pinkish particles like glitter. The blue light, now the same size, was pulsing gently. They moved over the top of each other, same size and shape, fitting perfectly together.

"That is beautiful. What's that?"

"That's your soul."

She looked closer. Why was it joined to the other one like that?

"I knew, at some level, when you told me you came through my portal. You shouldn't have been able to enter. Because, you see, portals are an old, old magic that enabled us to capture and bring humans back to our world. We no longer use them for that, thank the Five. They are called *dos sel doorii* in our language as they are designed to let only two souls through. First, your sister came through. Then I entered, to accompany her back. Some magic remained on the spot. You were only able to come through as your soul is tethered to mine."

"DON'T I HAVE ANY FREE will, then? Can't I choose what I do?" Soul mates, she thought. That was not a part of The Plan. What did that really mean? The phrase was cast around a lot in her world, the backbone of rom coms and influencer hashtags.

There were times when telling the truth seemed physically painful for him, and this was one of those times. He swallowed hard. "You can choose."

"I can choose. But what? I'd never have a good relationship? I'd be struck down dead? What happens if I don't play your game?"

"It's your soul to do with as you wish. And it's not a game," he said. "I didn't believe it for a long while, either."

"That's not an answer," she said.

"Do you think soulmates are common? We'll have to be apart for a while but I promise I'll find my way for us to be together. If you'll have me, we can be handfast right now." He magicked a ribbon out of nowhere and held his hand out. "All it takes is to give me your hand, Char—." He paused. "What is your name?"

"It's Cara," she said, with a smile.

What had she done? She'd given this guard, this warrior of the fae, this member of the cruel royal family, her name. She'd done it, without thinking twice, because she trusted him, fully and completely, with her life.

Men did not make great declarations of love to her. They didn't stay around for breakfast, let alone to be in a relationship.

"Do you not think you're worthy of this sort of love? I know you. I'm not going anywhere."

She looked up, sharply. He seemed to see through her. Perhaps she was the one who had left before they could leave her. Perhaps she was the one who was afraid.

She clasped his warm hand in hers, heart beating fast.

He wrapped the ribbon around their wrists and closed his hand over it. "I hope I can live up to your trust."

His eyes darkened and he leaned towards her for the kiss, lips pressing hers in a soft and gentle promise.

THE DOOR SLAMMED OPEN and wind pushed at them from all directions, making it hard for Cara to stand as they broke apart. Two fae guards loomed over them.

Hands held them firmly and they were marched up the path around the side of the well.

Cara opened her mouth to say something when she stumbled but Aeban shushed her. They didn't see anyone else on their journey upwards, and Cara felt it was ominous. Where was everyone?

The guards let them into a small chamber, then turned to leave. "We'll announce your arrival."

She turned to him. "What now? How are you going to get us out of this one?"

He shook his head. "There's no way to portal out of here. Listen, this is a side chamber to the main hall. We're going to be in front of everyone. Let's make it harder for them."

He passed his hand over her face. A warm, fuzzy feeling like mild intoxication crept over her skin. She looked down and saw that she was wearing a long cloak and dark green dress, with silver heels.

"A disguise?"

"Just be polite. And don't say anything." He said through his teeth.

Cara opened her mouth to say something, but the double doors opened silently inward.

The two guards stepped in to walk uncomfortably close to them, so that she could smell their sweat and the faint aroma of sweet wine. It was the same long hall as before, with huge, elegant columns, entwined with beautiful vines. Now it was set up with long tables and chairs all around. People were standing or sitting in small groups, chatting silently. They were guided towards a raised area in the centre with two long wooden dining tables. Again, the room fell silent.

The queen's voice rang out across the hall. "Aeban, my darling. It's a little rude to arrive home without seeing your mother. Where is the human witch?"

Cara's blood froze in her veins, but she somehow remembered to keep breathing and keep putting one foot in front of the other.

Aeban inclined his head. "Your majesty," he said, his speech measured. "I confess that if you cannot see her in the hall, there is not much I can do."

Cara looked up, sharply, impressed with his wit. He hadn't lied, per se.

The queen was nonplussed. "We saw you arrive with her. But it doesn't matter, we'll find her."

They really didn't recognise her at all. Had her whole appearance been glamoured to look like someone else?

Alawynn stood up as they came closer. "Late," he cried. "And not dressed for the occasion."

Cara made sure her face was showing no emotion. Ugh, he was an insufferable little twit. And he wanted to marry her sister?

The queen clapped her hands. "Enough. You know better than to give such an outburst. Well, we may as well get started. There's more time for business later."

The guards ushered them over to some chairs.

Nodding his head in agreement, the king stood up. "Thank you for coming, everyone. The realm welcomes you to the great Alder. We invite you all to enjoy the hospitality of The Vernal Court, while we pay tribute to the Five. May they return to our realm. The ball doesn't end until the ceremonial opening. Well, that's my part done." He lifted his goblet and a little wine splashed out.

The three flute players began a song that started off in a haunting melody. Three drummers brought their instruments in and started in a low beat.

When the beat changed, people started to dance, bringing a partner up with them. Cara watched them, dressed in silks and taffeta of all colours; dark purples and reds, bright turquoise to the most delicate pinks and greens. It was like ballroom dancing in their world, but perhaps less stiff and formal. When they all twirled together, it was as mesmerising as pinwheel fireworks on a cold winter's night.

One woman with dark skin had a beautiful silver suit that shone like a rainbow. Her partner, a much-taller, golden-skinned woman with hair like ropes, was dancing, her legs sliding along the floor in a sensuous manner that Cara couldn't look away from.

"Will you?" Aeban took her firmly by the hand and they went to an open space on the floor. She tried to protest.

"There is nothing much else for us to do. You just follow my lead. Don't fight," he said, placing one hand on the small of her back. With the other, he intertwined his fingers between her fingers.

She swallowed. This realm was so very strange. They were basically arrested and brought into a ballroom, where nobody seemed to care what they did next.

He led her backwards in slow steps. He turned and expected her to do the same.

"This is where we change partners," he said. "Just reach out, take their hand, then follow their lead. Look, it's Lord Azul. He'll be fine."

She managed to follow along but almost collapsed with relief when she got back to Aeban. He tucked her close to him, his fingers resting lightly in the middle of her back. She placed her cheek on his shoulder and could feel the warmth of his skin through his thin shirt.

Over his shoulder, the woman was dragging her leg up her partner's leg, then she put her head back and lazily drew her arm up her body and dangled it over her head.

"I'm surprised that's allowed with all your rules."

"She's a siren," he said, although he hadn't looked behind him. "She does get a little leeway. Although I know she was banned from the court for around fifty years."

"I'd say she'll be getting banned again," Cara said, raising her eyebrows.

"Nah. They need the sirens right now."

At one point, Aeban twisted her around so that she was facing outwards, his arms wrapped around her. "They're watching us," he said, his breath tickling her ear. "Move your leg with mine."

"I want to turn back around," she hissed, while trying to smile.

He placed his foot next to hers and pushed her leg back with force. So she stepped on his foot as hard as she could and when he let go, she turned back around.

"Just play along, Charming. Your life's in the balance here," he whispered into her ear.

"I do understand that," she whispered back. "Even if I don't understand anything else about this place. Luckily, I'll be out of here soon. What's your plan anyway?"

"Under our laws, the doors are locked until the dance is over. No one can portal in or out. That's why no one is too worried about us. I'll be able to draw magic after this to create a portal." He drew one hand down her hair, tenderly. "And don't write this place off so fast."

"Oh, I'm getting out of here, alright. There are way too many rules and they seem to change on a whim. But don't think you're getting out of here that easily. You attacked a guard, remember?"

"Shhh," he said.

DURING DINNER, THEY were seated at the foot of the table, near to the giant lion statues at the foot of the columns.

Cara eyed the queen, supremely smug, surrounded by her fawning lords and ladies. "They knew that you were coming back here, didn't they?" she whispered.

"Yes," he agreed, after he had carefully chewed his mouthful.

"But why? How were they so sure?"

"Well, apart from the fact that we get weaker the longer we're away... I've got a life waiting for me here," he mumbled.

"What life? Your family? You seem to disagree with everything they stand for."

"I disagree with their methods," he said, with a half grin. "I know you think me cowardly. But I have been doing what I could."

After dinner, people milled around. Cara and Aeban walked over to the drinks table. People eyed them curiously but Aeban didn't seem to notice.

Cara patted her hair. "This feels sort of like playing music while the Titanic is going down," she said.

Aeban looked at her as if he was concerned about her state of mind.

"Oh, don't worry. All I'm saying is it feels a little surreal."

"Oh, it is," he agreed. "Eyes up. Look who is coming over."

The queen, walking slowly in a huge dress, pale pink this time, approached them. Prince Alawynn kept trying to walk a pace ahead of her.

"My son," the queen said. "I'm overjoyed that you brought Veda with you tonight. It's lovely to see you two together, again."

Cara jerked. Who was Veda?

"Of course," Aeban answered, smoothly.

"It seems that you two are getting along well," Alawynn said with a smirk. "Mummy will be pleased."

Aeban said nothing.

"How are you faring, Veda?" the queen asked her.

"Well, thank you," she said, trying to mimic the strong and sultry voice of the faerie women she'd seen. Her blood chilled in her veins.

"Leave her be," Aeban said to his mother, who passed onto the next group.

"Who's Veda?" Cara hissed, as they walked over to the side.

He snorted. "She's a daughter of one of the powerful families. She's just lost her mother, The Lady Venera, and you kind of yelled at the queen about it." She could tell he was grinning, despite the seriousness of the topic.

"Oh," Cara said, embarrassed. "Some might react that way to grief, possibly?"

He led her back onto the dance floor and this time, she didn't struggle quite so much.

"The queen has always tried to push us together. Veda is from one of the high families. It would be a political alliance. That's why they were all crowing over you, or her, rather. Happy that we were spending time together."

"And you... like the way she looks? You did disguise me as her, after all." She looked at him from beneath her lashes.

"This has to be some sort of human trap," Aeban grumbled. "I shouldn't have told you that we cannot lie." He was silent for a moment. "I simply disguised you as her because I knew she wouldn't be at the ball. So there wouldn't be a double up. She was someone I used to know. You're mine."

Chapter 17

Aeban

His hand rested on the small of her back, his fingers itching to move over her skin. When the drums began, his body knew the steps of the dance like he knew the great tree. But although he remained calm, he watched his family.

This was a dangerous situation. He couldn't overpower this many of his people, especially not without his bow. He felt the lack of it like he wasn't wearing a jacket. If it was him alone, he'd take the punishment, that would undoubtedly be meted out, like a warrior. But it wasn't, now, and it never would be again.

He twirled her around, enjoying the way her eyes widened and her lips parted when she was taken by surprise. And everything took her by surprise. Everything brought the spark to her librarian's curious eyes.

Long ago, he'd been hopeful, working in the library, the destinarium sparkling above him. He remembered the feel of the cool stone under him as he worked late into the night, perfecting the manuscript with the help of Gwyneth and Fennen. The mushroom lanterns were losing their brightness and his eyes ached. Once he finished writing the last piece of description with a flourish, he looked up. He remembered that they all exchanged stares, feeling that this was something different, something momentous.

Gwyneth folded her arms. "You can do the offering. It's been too much work for them to reject it. I think I should flee forever if they do." She always was a little dramatic.

He remembered snatching the paper up. It felt so flimsy and delicate. The paper had seemed to float as if he could snatch it back, then suddenly it was gone.

No celebration rang out from the group. Aeban sat at the desk, chin on his hand. His mother and father had arrived in the library shortly afterwards.

"Tell us about this. Our advisors say it will be very useful. It might even be the invention of the decade."

"It's called ossilia, mother. It will simultaneously strengthen our kingdom and help with the problem of where to put our dead. It's a lichen. We could plant it in a field where there has been a battle. Then after a certain amount of time, the field would be fertile again. Where's the queen?"

"She's not the queen yet. Will it be expensive, though?"

"In my opinion, that's the best part. It requires very little magen energy."

That was the last time he called her mother. He was very young back then. It was a time before his aunt had gone missing on the morning of her coronation, before his mother had taken the throne. Before his mother had made the announcement that his aunt had been struck by a terrible curse, and was being kept downtree. Before he'd heard his aunt speak the prophecy.

He shrugged his shoulders, uncomfortable. He wasn't to know that the lichen would end up being used to strengthen the tree with the *literal skulls of their enemies*. There was no way of knowing that. But if you've been a part of the malice, even a very small part, you can still name it. In fact, it's your duty.

This whole cursed situation was like a ground battle. If you were losing, you could swing your sword and loose as many arrows as you liked, lost in the confusion. But it wasn't until you took flight that you could see the whole picture. He'd been trying to work within the existing rules for so long. Perhaps it was worth changing tack completely.

He was going to steal the Magen.

"SORRY," AEBAN SAID to her. "I have to do this. You'll be fine." He pulled away from her, walked calmly over to the chest beside the throne and moved, quick as a flash to take the solitary object inside. He strolled back to her, acting confident.

"What are you doing? Did you steal some silver?"

"Not quite," he said, beckoning her closer. He opened his hand. It was a shiny pot, embossed with pictures. She leaned forward to see, her eyes opening wide.

"Is that the Chalice? Did you just... take it?"

"No one cares. As part of the ceremony for these dances, the Magen is brought into the hall. Everything is locked up for the entire time and there are no weapons allowed. It's supposed to be a festival honouring the old gods."

He hid his hands behind his back as someone approached.

"May I cut in, Lady Veda?" It was Alawynn, offering his hand to Charming.

She hesitated and he nodded to tell her to go ahead. Breathing though his nose, he watched them move off. Alawynn had never shown the slightest interest in Veda. Until now that he thought Aeban was interested in her. Typical Smellawynn.

Eyes turned to follow them. Well, he supposed it took the focus away from him for a while. He made himself take a breath.

Chapter 18

Cara

What was he doing? Cara cast a glance over at Aeban, trying to ignore the sweaty hands of the prince.

"It appears your mind is elsewhere, Lady," the prince said. "What do you look for that I cannot provide?"

"Stimulating conversation," she said, before thinking.

Aeban took out the Chalice and spoke some words over it.

Alawynn whipped her around so that he was facing Aeban. "What would stimulate you? Battle stories?"

She noticed him looking interested in what his brother was doing and had to get him facing the other way. She kicked off her shoe and it went flying through the air, much higher than she'd thought. When it landed with a thunk, it was not a dark, silver heel but a plain, old, brown sneaker.

Alawynn stared at it. She could almost see his mind working.

"Who is our Chamberlain?" he asked her, silver-grey eyes hard and cold.

"What a strange question," she said. Her pulse raced as she tried to remember. Aeban had told her this. "Er, Fennen. It's Fennen."

His hands tightened. "Who is the cursed Herald?"

Alright, she didn't know this. "You're hurting me."

Cara looked to Aeban, who was still speaking words over the magen. One corner of the hall went from light, elegant wood to twisted, knobbly wood. Black dots ran over it and thick lichen covered the beams. How long would it be until someone noticed?

The glamour pulled back until it got to where the royal family were sitting. The table was covered in dust and cobwebs hung from the corners. The food piled on platters on the tables changed to piles of ashes and twigs and the people sitting around the table wore rags. Gasps and chatter rose from the people sitting around the edges of the hall.

The elegant lion statues became scaly gargoyles with mean eyes that rubbed their hands together. Someone screamed.

Alawynn let her go as he searched for the source of the commotion.

"It's the human witch," the queen cried, standing up.

Cara realized that her glamour must have gone as well. The two guards looked confused but grabbed Cara by the arm.

Aeban was still murmuring and pulling the glamour off the hall.

The queen looked from the corner to the table to the king. "Stop! Stop him!"

One of the guards let go of Cara and grabbed Aeban, wrestling the Chalice from him. "It's too late, your majesty," he said, supremely sarcastic. "Now, everyone can see what you've been hiding." He pointed up.

Through the lichen, white forms were visible. They were bones, Cara realised, sticking out of the framework. Goddess.

Cara looked at Aeban to see what he would do next, but he swayed alarmingly.

"What is the matter?" she asked.

He must have drawn too much magic in order to remove the glamour. There was no getting out of it this time.

The guards brought them to the high table. "Sit," the one holding her said, pressing her down to the ground.

Prince Alawynn shook his head at his brother. "Always dragging yourself down to look righteous, eh, *little* brother? It cost you the throne once."

"You would have left Fennen to die."

"Quiet." One word from the queen silenced both of them. "It's fine to have a fling, but we're too different. We fly, we're magnificent and we make miracles. You wriggle over the earth, multiplying, pillaging. Your kind are as fleeting and changeable as the spring wind and as absorbed in your own problems as the weeping cowvane."

"The fates will it," Aeban murmured.

The flash in the queen's eyes made Cara look away. She stopped to adjust her clothes, which were half rags, where the glamour had been pulled away. She drew herself up, terrible, implacable.

"Good luck if you think you're some destined lovers. Divination is a dead art, for a reason," the queen said. Turning to the rest of the room, she raised her voice. "He orchestrated all of this so that he could challenge the throne. You'll all see that travesty of our customs righted."

"Science," he muttered.

The queen continued on her tirade. "You've all heard the rumours he spread. Trying to bring discord to our realm of peace."

"What does she mean?" Cara whispered.

"She's been suspicious of her own family for a long time," he murmured. "Often the guilty are."

A murmuring and shuffling came from the crowd. Cara craned to see what everyone was looking at.

It was a garden gnome, from his appearance. He was about two feet tall and he was dressed in a gorgeous purple suit, but his shirt buttons were undone. He spoke with a surprisingly loud, deep voice that rung out around the high-ceilinged hall.

"Your majesty, we've been your fiercest allies for as long as I can remember. But this is not right. Our captain is always loyal to the realm, while keeping all of the guard and the allies happy. I can't stand back and watch as you lambast him!" He blasted the doors open with a bang.

A silence so complete and dangerous followed this declaration.

"Now," Aeban whispered in her ear.

Cara hesitated for only a moment before raising the magic in her blood, feeling it build and grow. She sent sparks out to each corner of the room. One caught on the curtains and blazed up the side.

Aeban grabbed her and moved. Her legs struggled to keep up as he rushed like the wind. They crossed the room and went out the doors, down another hallway and stopped in an alcove.

"Are you alright?" she asked Aeban, as he leaned back against the wall. "I don't understand half of what happened out there."

"I am. What about you?" He passed his hand over her, removing the glamour. "That's better." He caressed her chin.

She nodded.

"Later," he said.

Chapter 19

Cara

They raced down the hallway, hand in hand. Cara turned a corner and she smacked straight into someone.

"Serena." Cara pulled her into a tight hug, inhaling her scent. She smelled of plants and happiness and summer evenings. After a long moment, she pulled apart, keeping her at arm's length.

"I knew you'd find my message, nerd."

"Viola! You're lucky I remembered that."

Aeban bowed low to her. "I'm glad to find you well. My apologies for our first meeting. But we do not have time for chatter." He sent magic out towards a plant that was creeping slowly towards them, its spiky tendrils questing around the walls, hungrily. It shrank back immediately.

He ushered them down a hallway and into what seemed to be a small chapel. "Stay in here. I'll go and check if it's safe to portal through a mirror."

Cara sat on a wooden stool. She couldn't keep the smile off her face, looking at Serena.

"How did you get here?" Serena asked her.

"I followed you through the portal. They locked me up when I arrived in a garden prison at the top of the tree. I got out, thanks to that guy. Spent two days at home. Then we came back to get you."

Serena gaped. "You've done all of that? Are you and him together?"

"You might say that," she said, with a secret smile. There would be time, later, for all of that. "What were you doing?"

"I'm currently trying to convince the prince that I should open a little school teaching about mortals. They are dreadfully misinformed about some things." She paused. "He's bloody awful, Caz."

"So why did you want to stay here?" Cara asked. "I couldn't believe it."

There was a long pause, during which water dripped somewhere. There appeared to be a water clock in the monument in the corner.

Serena let out a breath. "Imagine if you had been running a race all day. Like the sports days at school, remember? But you're doing it now, as an adult. You ran your hardest on a hot sunny day. Now you constantly need to drink water. You're hungry but you can't process food. Your jaw hurts, your eye sockets ache, nerves jangle. Every single muscle burns."

"Yeah, I know you're in pain," Cara said, not wanting to hear it because she hated that she couldn't help. "Are you alright at the moment?"

"But you can't really understand. Sorry, but you can't." Her eyes flicked away. "The first time I was allowed out to explore, I went with a guard and another mortal. The gardener... The Whisperer, he is called. I suppose that we would call him a gardener, although I get the feeling he's more like a... shepherd." She fumbled for the word, as if finding the word insufficient. "He grows plants from all over the realm. He creates them like he's modelling with clay. I was, like, swearing at the amazing things I saw."

"I can imagine," Cara said, drily.

"A leafy umbrella-shaped plant that causes rain to fall from it, so that there are tiny miniature worlds growing around each one. A flower that smells exactly like the best memories of your childhood, if you can believe it." She shook her head. "So it sort of smelt, to me, like popcorn, candy floss, and horses. The town fair, I think. Also there was a bush that grows to five metres tall, and looks like dragons are emerging from it. There was a vine that they kept caged. I'm not sure why. Each week there were new plants. Always something different to see."

"It does sound amazing."

"But I was getting so excited about seeing everything that I walked a lot further than I realized. I got breathless, like I do, and my legs turned to jelly. Well, the guard just floated me along, no question at all. Absolutely no effort for him, it seemed. And no judgement, either. The food there actually gave me energy instead of my body using it all just to digest and sleep felt like floating in a warm bath. My illness wasn't something that couldn't be talked about. It wasn't something that's a bit wrong. No one said I should try to 'get a proper job', like our neighbour says. There's a certain freedom in acceptance."

Cara could see why her sister would have liked that. In this realm, it did seem to be part of their customs to help people that needed it. In their own world, that had maybe gotten lost somewhere along the way.

"At first, I thought I was better. But I think I just felt happier, maybe because it was all new. Like being on holiday."

"I think it might be part of their glamour." She explained about what Aeban had shown her. "This world is really nothing like what you see."

Serena whistled. "What the—."

"I know."

Aeban popped his head around the door. "Alright, come on," he said. "If we go around the corner, we can use the mirror in the greenhouse."

Serena whispered, "I think those might be the most words he's ever spoken to me."

"Tell me about it," Cara said, wryly.

They crept along the corridor, into a doorway and down a curving earthen ramp. They passed a kitchen where delicious smells were wafting out. Aeban pulled her along again and they entered a larder with shelves of cheeses and jars upon jars of preserves. They went through a huge glass door and they were in the glasshouse.

The heat and smells of the glasshouse hit her immediately, bringing back a familiar longing for home, but this was no orderly room with tidy shelves of plants in pots. It was like a slice of The Auld Forest, complete with hanging vines, toadstools and moss. A huge cloud hung under the ceiling, almost like she could touch it.

"You have to look at these," Serena said. There was a plant with delicate flowers that were actually snowflakes. She could feel the chill from it. Garden goals. She reached out towards a shrub that seemed to have dark blue paint dripping from its broad leaves.

"That one will give you a tattoo if you get close enough to it," Serena put in.

Cara pulled her hand back. She looked ahead to where Aeban was already at the other end of the long room.

"Really? There was no closer mirror than that? Let's go, sis." They made their way around the plants, carefully. It felt like everything was holding its breath in the heavy, damp air.

Serena stopped to catch her breath, hand on her chest. "Maybe I wanted... to think I was better so much that I thought the very air here was magical. Full of healing power. But perhaps, it was just that they helped me at every turn, without me asking or feeling guilty. And I thought I wanted, needed, a family. But he was cruel to me. And a family might be nice, some day... But not like that. Not him. What I really wanted was acceptance..."

She had gone very pale.

"Hey, head up," Cara said to her. "It must be the humidity in here."

Serena took a sharp breath in.

"In. Out. Slowly," she said, but Serena shook her head, face whiter than normal.

Cara turned around and saw a stand of dark red trees that definitely wasn't there before. But 'trees' was not a sufficient word to describe the heaving mass of purple, burgundy twisting vines and storm of clacking twigs.

"It's the one from the... cage," she said.

Suddenly, Aeban was there, whipping past her to stand in front of the mass of angry sticks. He held his hands up and started to sing, voice pitched low.

The clacking became less frequent and finally, the trees shuffled off.

Cara and Serena were standing there with their mouths open.

"Come on." Aeban strode past them. "It's a lullaby," he threw over his shoulder. "The plant is an insomniac. It gets really angry when it hasn't slept."

"How did you know what to do?"

"I invented it," came the low growl.

The door slammed open behind them and one of the guards appeared.

"Time to go."

They ran along the greenhouse, dodging plants and hanging vines until they saw the glint of the mirror, from behind a small sapling. It was only after Aeban ushered them through in silence and they landed in the cobbled street that Cara felt she could breathe again.

Chapter 20

Cara

They dropped Serena back into the loving care of Donil and Maerie, leaving her with a flagon of warming tea and a plate of emerald cakes. Aeban gave the couple a threatening order to look after Serena, where bones and grinding were mentioned more than once.

Aeban took Cara's hand and they walked down the middle of the street. "We'll have to wait until I can rest enough to be able to make a portal to send you both back."

"Alright."

"Still peaceful enough out here," he said.

"How come you're not worried that they will come and get you?"

"Trust me, they will be running around like pheasants in a scatterpat. We'll have a little time."

She threw him a quizzical look, but waved her hand to dismiss the unusual simile.

"Will you tell me what was happening back there? I want to know all the gory details."

"There was a prophecy," he started, as if that explained everything. "That the throne would fall in this decade. Only the queen and I heard it. Or so I thought. But someone wrote a ballad and people whispered about it. I wouldn't say a movement but it was persistent. Then the festival sprang up from nowhere. The queen has often implied that I'm behind it."

"But the throne hasn't fallen? I thought there'd be more" — she made a motion with her hand as if she was stabbing someone — "and there's no one new on the big seat."

"Oh, the throne has fallen, alright. This will be the biggest scandal the powerful families have seen in decades. It will sow the first doubts in their mind about the royals and their way of doing things, if not drop their trust in them, entirely. The people have seen their allies undermine the royals, right in front of their eyes, and a show of no confidence from one of their own."

"Wow," she breathed.

As they walked, she was wondering how it was going to be back in Ledstow. She and Aeban were so different. "I work a lot. My coven needs me and so does my sister."

"And I'll wait for you."

"I don't really know how to be in a relationship," she blurted.

"Neither do I. But we'll work it out."

SOMETHING HAD BEEN gnawing at Cara and she placed her hand on his arm. "We have to go and see Nate. Before I go. Please."

"Who?"

"He is one of the other prisoners. I have to get his details so I can check on his wife. It's the absolute least I can do for him as he's... never going to be leaving."

"Of course. Can I get a moondew first? It's been a long night." He gestured helplessly towards the tavern.

She nudged him in the side. "There will be many nights for moondew."

They landed in the prison courtyard, which was eerily deserted. The silver light turned the contemplation pool to liquid mercury and wind rustled the leaves.

"Over here, I think." She walked towards one of the cells. "No, this one."

"Oh, I know who you mean." Aeban moved the branches apart so they could look inside. "I call him Rosewood."

There was no one in there, just some hollowed out earth in the moonlight.

"Oh! I was sure this one was right." She put her hands on her hips.

But a great light appeared behind them. Cara put her hands up to shield her eyes, trying to make out what was approaching. It appeared to be a man. A man who was laughing a rich, deep laugh.

Aeban bowed low. What was he doing now?

"The great god Lumbris," he said, in an awed voice.

Cara's breath caught. The man stopped in front of them. He reached out and shook their hands in turn, with a firm grip. He had the strong upper body and shoulders of an Olympic swimmer but was at least a foot taller than Aeban. He had long, thick, black hair.

"It is me. You've shown great care for this man. Both of you. Aeban, you begged your mother for mercy for him in the court. That took bravery. How proud Randolynn would be. And Cara, you were a great friend to him when it felt like all was lost. To me, rather."

"Was it you all along?" The question burst out of her, before she could stop it.

Lumbris inclined his head, long hair falling over his face. "I have a penchant for costumes, I'm afraid. It's a great way to see how people truly behave, when they are least expecting to see a god. A great way to see who they really are. Can I do anything for you?"

At their blank looks, he smiled. "This is your chance. In each other, I know you've both found a safe place to land, already. So come on, what are your wishes?"

"No wishes for me," said Cara, shaking her head.

"I'd like to go and live in the human realm for a while," Aeban said.

"Granted, young one. I've been watching for far too long. All five of us have been hanging back, waiting for a time when we could step in. But never think that no one's listening. When I see a little change just beginning, that's when I can come and help. And I think I'll have more to do with both of you."

He put a hand out towards them, whether in farewell or blessing Cara wasn't sure.

"And now, I think I'll take up a good spot in the court and watch things implode." He laughed again.

THE GLOW FADED AND an echo of a laugh reverberated around them. For once, Aeban was the dumbstruck one. He put one arm around Cara's waist and lifted into the air, powerful wings taking them up in the air as they made their way out of the tree.

Cara saw huge chambers between the branches filled with people. She heard singing. But her mind was occupied.

By the time they landed at the inn, all of the questions Cara had were ready to burst out. "So, are you telling me that that was one of your gods? The very same one in the legend?"

Aeban said nothing as they walked down the alley.

"Did Nate Blackwood never exist? Did Lumbris make up all those details? Is Nate's wife a real person? I'm really confused."

"I've often heard that the gods challenge us from time to time. We'll never know the exact reasons for their actions." He turned to her when they reached the inn, placing a light kiss on her forehead. "When I first met you, I actually thought you might have been the goddess Feisia incarnate. She appears as a woman in the villages who thirsts for knowledge, perhaps with a strange herbal wisdom. She's pretty feisty, too. You can see why I thought that."

"But I'm just me," Cara said. She leaned against him.

"Cara," he agreed. "Do you know that I've known your name since you first saw your sister?" he asked. "I also saw it on a scroll in your house."

She thought back and realised he was right. Her sister had said her name. That could have gone really badly, she reflected. But her soul was safe with him.

"You asked me for it, so it was my choice whether to give it you."

He nodded. "Yes."

Sometimes a book shelved in the wrong place found its way into the perfect hands.

❧

THE END

Author's Note

I hope you enjoyed A Twist of Faerie as much as I enjoyed writing it. I dedicate it to all the bookish girls, who know that sometimes there's only one thing to be done: rearranging the bookshelves. This is a spin-off featuring Cara, who is the librarian from my Musical Mayhem series of witchy cosy mysteries set in Ledstow. If you liked the book, please consider reviewing it. I will be eternally grateful.

Also by the Author

Musical Mayhem Series
Murder for a Song
Death and a Duet
Treble Death

Redferne Witches Series
Brand of Magic
Boundless Magic
Murmurs of Magic
Breaking into Magic

Cast of Characters

❖ Cara Jennings - Librarian first, then human witch, portal-traveller and pragmatic maker of Plans

❖ Serena Jennings - Part-time graphic designer and headstrong fan of black comedy

❖ Aeban se Randolynn (AY Bahn) - Captain of the Royal Guard, he is a fae who is Very Tall, equal parts tortured, dutiful and magnetic

❖ Alawynn se Randolynn (Al a WIN) - Heir to the Vernal Throne, also known as Smellawynn

❖ Queen Talynn s'Argonne (TA Lin) - Holder of Many Titles, Very Important Person etc etc

❖ Prince Menuel se Randolynn (MEN Yel) - Husband to the queen, in charge of Bringing Her Down a Peg or Two

❖ Ynore se Haira (Ee NOR) - Owns a tavern in Bracken, perpetually stressed mother

❖ Garin se Galadynn (GA Rin) - Herald to the Court, Loudmouth

❖ Fennen s'Amor (FEN In) - A half-centaur Official

Chamberlain and Head Librarian

❖ Venera se Wemila (Ve NEAR a) - Now-deceased matriarch of one of the Powerful Families

❖ Veda se Wemila (VEE Da) - Daughter of the above and unwitting matchmaking object of the queen

❖ Maerie se Halda and Donil se Halda (MARE Ee and DO Nil) - Owners of the Hog & Steel Inn

❖ Menele se Baran (MEN a Lay) - A fae guard who always appears at the wrong place and time

❖ Tuel s'Olann (Tyew ELL) - The queen's half-naiad psychic handmaiden

❖ Murrell Blackshield (Ma RELL) - Fierce warrior gnome from the Lowlands who hates politics almost as much as wearing clothes

❖ Lord Yan Azul (YAHN) - Werewolf shifter ambassador from the Wolflands

❖ Lady Dreia de Maine (DRAY a) - Naiad ambassador